A very special thanks to:

Huey Rawls, for your immensely generous support, and being a brother whose bond is stronger than blood.

Margarita Seroshtan, for the time and talent you selflessly gave.

John Charitonov, for composing the song which sparked my thoughts to write this book.

Vitaly Kibenko, for being there for me when no one else would, even when this book was merely an idea.

Brandon Wood, for pushing me to write like a true author, much like yourself.

Alex Gorbonov, for your efforts to fine tune the finished product to perfection.

Becky Kulakevich, for listening as I poured out my thoughts and for helping me write a portion of the book.

Kylee Date, for your encouragement, and staying up late with me to help overcome my writers block.

Robert Filimonchuk, for understanding, even when you didn't understand, and for every single prayer you've prayed over this book.

And to those who contributed to the crowdfunding campaign,

THE PRODIGAL SON – EVERY DREAM HAS A BEGINNING:

Budai, Esther

Cheban, Samuel

Curtean, Daniel and Zinaida

Eskelin, Susan

Filimonchuk, Margarita

Fortygin, Alex and Victoria

Fortygin, Eduard and Svetlana

Moore, Gene

Gelzer, Josh and Anya

Lauder, Jonathan

Moraru, Slaveck

Prikhodko, Angelina

Propp, Manuela

Saasen, Brittany

Smalley, Andrew

Tseona, Solomiya

Venturine, Troy

Yagolnikov, Vladislav

Yudich, Dennis

Theparableofgabriel.com

The Prodigal Son

—

The Parable of Gabriel

(This Is A Thirteen Day Excerpt From Gabriel's Life)

Based on the movie in my head

Chapter 1

I ronically, it was a sunny morning in not-so-sunny Seattle. The automated blinds opened to illuminate the room as a melodic 7:00am alarm set the scene to a peaceful morning. A lawn mower rumbled its engine outside, and from the kitchen came the smell of blueberry crepes, but Gabriel wasn't having it. Much like every morning, Gabriel started by snoozing his alarm, and much like every morning, he found himself looking like total chaos.

Gabriel wasn't a heavy sleeper, but he was a heavy dreamer. Some nights he would fall asleep firmly on his back, only to wake up lying horizontally on his bed—twisted like a stick of licorice. His natural brown hair matched perfectly with his eye color, and his slender legs hung off the queen size bed with a sock on one foot and the other foot bare.

From the bathroom came roaring vocalizations. It was Gabriel's older brother, Samuel. "Handsome Sam," so nicknamed for his luscious blond hair, penetrating blue eyes, and teeth-whiter-than-sour-cream smile. Competence, maturity, and ferocious charm weren't the only positives about Sam, he also happened to be the head of operations and lead ambassador for his father's company 'Urban Post' street-paper. No doubt about it, Sam was next in line to become CEO of Urban Post—the heir to the throne, the runner up. This didn't impress Gabriel one bit.

When Sam was finished with his vocal audition in the shower, he knocked on Gabriel's door to wake him. Gabriel sprung out from his prolonged slumber and trailed over to the bathroom. The combination of extreme sleepiness and sudden rush of blood to the head explained why he had mistakenly squeezed anti-acne cream onto his toothbrush instead of toothpaste. After contact was made between the "fix-my-face" cream and his tongue, it was lights on.

Once Gabriel's mouth was spick-and-span, he proceeded to feed his goldfish, Atlas. Nobody really knew how Atlas found its way into the house to begin with. It's almost as if a friend or relative had snuck it in and placed it somewhere inconspicuously, then grinned devilishly like they had just pulled off a bank heist in a cheesy 1980's cartoon. Gabriel had taken the liberty of adopting Atlas as his own. It just felt right, especially since Gabriel himself often felt misplaced, like he was born in the wrong era or perhaps the wrong family.

Gabriel finished feeding Atlas, then marked the day off on the family calendar. It was January 31st, and the reminder read, "Mom's Memorial." He hesitated to mark it, but after doing so, he resumed his morning routine. Sam was washing dishes when Gabriel walked past him. No contact was made, or any words exchanged between them, yet Gabriel was already annoyed. He did his best to ignore Sam, but Sam was the sort of person who took over any atmosphere that they were in; a real neck-turner in a crowded room.

"Aunt Betty wanted us to have a good breakfast," Sam said. Gabriel glanced peevishly at Sam while helping himself to a plate of blueberry crepes.

"When was the last time Aunt Betty's crepes tasted anything like Mom's?" Gabriel shrugged. Sam looked over his shoulder.

"You better not be like that tonight."

"Don't worry about me," Gabriel replied, blank-faced.

"I'm serious, Gabe. Everyone is going to be there so you better not show any attitude,"

Gabriel got up to make himself a cup of coffee, leaving his dirty plate on the table. "Look at this," Sam pointed at the plate, "Leaving all your crap behind and you haven't even been here five minutes."

"So clean it up," Gabriel retorted, "—if it bothers you so much."

"You're like... twenty years old. At least try to act your age."

"I don't know—I've never been this old before—so how could I act my age?" Gabriel smirked.

Sam shook his head disapprovingly as he continued washing the dishes.

"Your jokes aren't funny you know."

"Aha, they're actually pretty funny," Gabriel grinned slightly.

"No, they're not—actually."

Being the genius he thought himself to be, Gabriel decided to throw his fork into the sink from across the kitchen. The fork flew right past Sam and created a screeching noise as it crashed into the stainless-steel sink. Sam flinched like a cat being tossed into water.

"Dude! Really?" Sam dropped the plate he was wiping and looked at his wet shirt. "You really have nothing better to do?"

"Nope," Gabriel replied, laughing bitterly.

"Don't you have somewhere to be?"

Gabriel looked at the time. Suddenly realizing how late he was, he sprung out of his seat, not paying attention to the cup of coffee he still had in his hand. The beverage spilled all over his jeans and shirt. He fumbled around trying to level the cup.

"Wow, you suck," Sam chuckled.

Gabriel puffed and sprinted off to his room. His thundering footsteps echoed through seven-bedroom house. Grabbing every piece of clothing needed, Gabriel hurried to the door, slipping into his coat and pants as he made his way. Just then, a knock resounded through the house. Gabriel peeked through the window to see who it was. It was Aunt Betty, Gabriel's Mother's Sister, and maker of the infamous crepes. Gabriel threw his foot in the way of the door to stop it from opening.

"Gabey dear, is that you?" She asked, her voice muffled from behind the door. Stumbling and panicked, Gabriel struggled to pull his pants up before Aunt Betty came in.

"Oh my gosh, this is so embarrassing," Gabriel muttered to himself as he heard Sam laughing from the kitchen. "You aren't helping!" Gabriel shouted. He was now at the point of desperation as he was unable to get his zipper to close. The hurry, the pressure, the smell of those crepes, all of this was overwhelming Gabriel, and Aunt Betty's persistence was only making matters worse.

"I think there is something wrong with this door of yours," She said through a small crack in the door.

"Uh... yes—yes there is! Let me just fix it real quick and you can just... stay out there," Gabriel stalled Aunt Betty. Movements such as Gabriel's could only be seen from a low budget circus clown, and he certainly looked the part.

"Oh dear, let me help you with this door of yours," Aunt Betty offered.

"No! It's okay," Gabriel shouted just as Aunt Betty pressed her shoulder into the door, swinging it wide open and pushing Gabriel back a yard. Gabriel swiftly yanked the zipper up with all his might, and closed his eyes.

"Oh my, are you okay?" Aunt Betty voiced her concern. Gabriel opened his eyes and noticed her standing in front of him and glaring back like she were a deer in headlights. Sam bursted out in laughter. Gabriel didn't acknowledge the question, or even the situation. He grabbed his keys and darted out of the house. "Will I see you tonight, sweetie?" Aunt Betty called out as Gabriel was speed walking away.

"Yeah, Auntie—I'll see ya," Gabriel replied as he got into his car.

Gabriel walked into his community college class a half an hour late and at the most cliché of moments, in the middle of reading time. He made way to his desk, trying to avoid eye contact with any of his peers. The teacher, Brian, walked up to Gabriel. His magnificent beard hung down from his chin and over Gabriel's desk like an ivy vine. Brian leaned his walking stick on Gabriel's desk and handed him the results from last week's test. When Gabriel looked at the test results, he noticed a beautifully bold "F" at the top of the page.

"Wait, an 'f?'" Gabriel asked, "I thought you were gonna give me that extra credit thingy." The class interrupted their studies and began observing the situation.

"The extra credit 'thingy' is already included," Brian explained.

"I—I stayed after class though, like what was the point then?" Gabriel complained. The class became silent and Brian gave Gabriel his infamous one-brow-raised stare. He took his little red pen of dream killing and placed a plus sign in front of the score.

"F-plus?" Gabriel asked out loud. The neighboring students giggled snottily but Gabriel wasn't fazed by it.

"Okay let's get back on track here, everybody," Brian announced as he limped back to his desk.

After class was dismissed, Gabriel approached Brian's desk. Brian was shuffling through a bundle of assignments.

"I don't want to hear about all the different reasons why I should let you take that test again," He said, chewing on a toothpick, "If you would have studied, then you would have passed."

"I was just gonna say thanks for the extra credit," Gabriel spoke quietly.

Brian lowered his glasses and looked at Gabriel. He sighed before saying, "I know you're smart. You've got so much brains in that head of yours."

"I know." Gabriel scratched the hairs under his ear.

"I know that you know, and that's really good—knowing is the first step, but if you don't start showing up—mentally showing up, where your mind is focused and you're paying full attention—then you won't get far," Brian lectured, "You're perfectly capable of passing this."

"I'll try," Gabriel sighed.

"What I think you should do is find something that motivates you," Brian suggested.

"That's—yep. That's what I need, you're totally right, and I'll get right on that." Gabriel said.

"Oh Gabriel—here, take this," Brian called out as Gabriel was walking away. "It won't get your grade up by much, but it'll get you past an F."

Gabriel took the folder that Brian held up, cracked a smile, then lifted his eyes up to Brian.

"You mean an F-plus?" Gabriel winked.

"Yes—get that done, okay?"

"Yes-sir!" Gabriel hurried out the classroom.

"Remember, I want you out of this class as much as you!" Brian shouted as Gabriel was already outside.

There was a cafe on campus that Gabriel frequented. The smell of chai tea and lavender permeated, reaching Gabriel's nose as soon as he stepped-foot inside. Most of the cafe had tall windows for walls, yet the gloom of the cloudy day brought a jaded feel to the over-all atmosphere.

"How's it going my dude?" the barista, a middle aged Latino named Gustavo, asked from behind the counter.

"I'm alright, let me get a six-shot today," Gabriel said, rubbing his eyes on his sleeve.

"Long day, bro?"

"Something like that—just have ton of homework to do and I need caffeine in my system, you know?"

"Yeah bro, Coffee is the mini—" Gustavo began quoting.

"—Vacation we all need every once in a while—I know," Gabriel finished.

"Aha enjoy, bro," Gustavo handed Gabriel his beverage.

"I will, thanks."

Gabriel sat down at his favorite spot, the long coffee bar that stretched along the floor-to-ceiling windows. As he waited for his laptop to boot up, he pulled out a black journal from his bag. Taking his time, Gabriel opened the journal and began flipping through the pages of art that he had drawn over the years. The art never failed to flood his mind with a wave of memories. He smiled, nearly tearing up, as he reminisced the times he drew the pictures; when joy came so easily, and the fear of expressing himself was nonexistent.

Gabriel reached a page, somewhere in the middle of the journal, where there was the last picture he ever drew. Several years ago, on a troubling evening in his attic room, Gabriel was sitting crisscross on his wool-blanketed bed near the window. Unsure of how to express his emotion, he touched a pencil to the center of the page of his journal and kept it there. He tried to understand why he was unable to draw anything when he heard Sam's thundering footsteps up the stairs. The door swung open and Sam said the words that Gabriel would never be able to let go.

"I think Mom is about to die."

That night Gabriel's worst fear came to life, his mother passed away. He gave up on expressing himself, and hasn't tried again since. There was no art that could adequately capture the emotion he felt when the very person that mattered most was now without a heartbeat. After all, his mother was the one that brought life to him, and with that life came an atmosphere that Gabriel felt comfortable dreaming in. He understood now why he gave up art; the fear that came forth from it made him think that if he draws, something terrible will happen again.

For his mother, life had always been about the moments that created their own memories. Day in and day out, she spoke of finding something worth pausing life for, and simply observing, listening, calmly breathing, and taking in the music that life creates when it's appreciated. Gabriel had a hard time finding that kind of freedom now. Still, somewhere deep in his murky depths, he knew he was a whimsical being; a curious kid eager to climb every tree.

Sitting there in that cafe, Gabriel glared at the dot feeling completely numb. It took a while before he could fully come back to himself. He thought maybe finishing the drawing now would somehow bring him closure. So he stayed there the remainder of the evening like time was nonexistent. Much like the night all those years ago, Gabriel couldn't get past that dot in the center of the page. When he got home he tried to get to his room as quietly as possible, hoping his father, Leon, who sat in the office by the front door, wouldn't bother him.

"Gabe," Leon said sternly. Gabriel paused, took a few steps back, and leaned his head into the office. Leon was wearing a pair of reading glasses that had a lanyard attached around his neck. He had a stony expression on his face, as he had most evenings, but this time it was slightly dourer than usual.

"Why weren't you here for the memorial?" Leon asked.

"Homework," Gabriel replied monotonously.

"Everyone was here—and you had Aunt Betty worried sick," Leon continued.

"I already told you, I had homework."

"Homework—until 10pm?" Leon puffed.

"Dad, I'm not a kid anymore."

"That's something only a kid would say," Leon muttered, his attention mostly focused on the paperwork and monitor before him.

Gabriel marched to his room, dropped his bag on the bedroom floor, and leaped into bed. He pulled out his phone and group-texted his two friends, "Blake" and "Noah."

Gabriel: *OMG my dad grrrr!!! Are we still on for the get together tomorrow?*

Blake: *Yeah buddy!*

Gabriel: *All right, Noah's place?*

Noah: *Nope! Can't do my house guys… and I don't wanna waste money at a restaurant either, let's go to our spot??*

Gabriel: *I'm down*

Blake: *That place smells like dead animals*

Gabriel: *Gross Blake*

Noah: *My house smells even worse right now lol*

Blake: *Noah it's you that smells bad, not your house*

Noah: *No your house smells bad… oh yeah, never mind… you don't have a house lol*

Blake: *You're**

Noah: *Actually in this case it's your**

Gabriel: *ANYWAY usual spot it is. G'night!*

Blake: *K*

Noah: *lol This is why I love you guys! Peace*

Chapter 2

Staring impatiently at the outdated classroom clock, Gabriel rested his chin against the palm of his hand and murmured, "Seriously… another two semesters of this?"

"Have something to say there?" Brian turned around and asked.

"This stuff is so literally pointless," Gabriel complained, letting his pencil drop on the worksheet.

"It's not pointless," Brian reassured.

"It totally is! The only reason it was useful for you was because you became a teacher," Gabriel reasoned.

Brian took his glasses off. "Let me ask you, do you remember when you first came into my class, and you expressed that you wanted to get out as quickly as possible?" Gabriel nodded yes. "Right, then. Just do your work and quit complaining."

"I know but—"

"No, you need to stop, Gabe," Brian interrupted despotically, "I want you to finish this class just as much as you do—it's why I am letting you take that extra credit. Which reminds me, have you finished it?"

"Not really," Gabriel shook his head.

For a moment, Brian watched Gabriel blank-faced. "Not really?" He questioned as he rubbed his hands together. Gabriel opened his mouth to reply, but Brian slowly turned away, walked over to the telephone on his desk, and began dialing.

"Class is now dismissed—please don't forget we have the courtyard study tomorrow so be prepared for that," Brian announced. He took one more look at Gabriel. "Hello, Lucy? Would you be able to leave the key out tonight?" Brian said into the telephone. Gabriel played with his pencil, trying not to show his nervousness. "Okay thank you—and uh—I'll lock up the place as per usual," Brian continued, "Alright. Thank you very much, Lucy," Gabriel suspected Brian and Lucy were lovers by the way Brian smiled coquettishly while talking with her. "Mm—buh-bye," Brian hung up. While waiting for a response, Gabriel had already thought of several excuses to get out of whatever was coming his way. Brian neared him. "So, this won't be until Friday," Brian began saying, "But it looks like we will have to get together at the library. Before then, I want you to finish the extra cred' I already gave you."

"Sounds like my kind of Friday night," Gabriel stated sarcastically.

"Don't give me that... come on." Brian shook his head. "You can go."

"I'm just joking," Gabriel replied, rushing out of the classroom.

"Yeah okay, I'll see you tomorrow, Gabe," Brian said, matching Gabriel's sarcastic tone, "Looking forward to Friday!"

Gabriel skipped out of the classroom like a kid going to school recess. He was walking to the cafe when the misty weather accelerated his pace. Soon the drizzle turned to deluge, causing Gabriel to turn from a light stroll to a sprint. As he neared the cafe, there were two girls about twenty yards away from him. The girls, like Gabriel, were also frantic to get indoors. The three of them ran inattentively to the cafe and collided at the front door like waves. In the frenzy of things, one of the girls tried to push the door open full force. Her momentum moved her entire body into the glass. Since the door didn't open in that direction, the only thing that moved was the girls face into the glass like dough being rolled into a pizza.

"Oh my g—are you okay?" Gabriel asked, trying to contain his laughter.

"Yeah I'm alright. My face broke the fall," the girl replied. Her dark and completely drenched hair swung, nearly slapping Gabriel in the face, as she turned to give her answer. The other girl stood back and lost control of her laughter. Gabriel thought he heard a half-ton grizzly bear roaring behind him; that was until he turned around and saw that it was only a sweet little blonde girl. The situation, mingled with the train-horn like laughter, put the three of them into unmitigated hysteria.

"What's going on here?" Gustavo yelled, before he recognized Gabriel. "You trying to break my doors, bro?"

He complained as he held the door open. "Come on, get in and try not to run into the front counter either."

"Sorry, it's just the rain," Gabriel said, still trying to swallow his giggles. The girls entered in first and went straight into the restroom. Gabriel came into the cafe after them, relieved that there were no customers inside who would have probably been disturbed by the ruckus.

"The usual," Gabriel stated, "Oh, and here's ten bucks to pay towards whatever those girls get."

"Please be more careful with the doors man," Gustavo grumbled "Do you know them?"

"No, I just ran into them, and uh… no pun intended there," Gabriel said, "Get it? —aha!"

"I do get it. It's just not funny after you try to break my cafe." Gustavo handed Gabriel a receipt.

"Alright man, I'm sorry. It won't happen again— hey, don't forget the ten bucks."

Gabriel took his drink over to a larger table. His intention was to pick a table with plenty of seating in hopes that the girls would join him. When the girls came out the restroom, they trailed over to Gustavo with their boots still dripping wet. Gabriel had been rehearsing how he was going to more formally introduce himself. It wasn't like him to interact with unfamiliar girls, but he figured he'd give it a shot. He looked over his shoulder as he could hear their slippery footwear squeak against the concrete floor. Although it was the rain outside that left Gabriel with wet hair, it may as well have been his nervous sweat.

"Just smile," Gabriel murmured to himself, "And show your teeth."

"Thanks for paying it forward," the girl with the dark hair said as she walked by.

"Great thanks," Gabriel replied, exaggerating his smile, "I mean… you're welcome."

"I'm sorry?" the girl asked.

"What?"

"I didn't hear what you said," The girl pulled her hair over her ear.

"Oh—I said you're welcome… is… what I said," Gabriel fumbled his words, hoping he hadn't already embarrassed himself too much.

"Well thanks, homie," she replied whimsically before continuing to the coffee bar by the window.

"Gah, I knew I should have just sat there," Gabriel said under his breath. "Hey, you guys uh—maybe wanna sit here?" he called out. The girls looked at each other and shrugged their shoulders. Gabriel quickly pulled out both seats and wiped the table with a napkin.

"So, I'm Gabriel."

"I'm Lily," the dark haired girl said. Gabriel stretched his hand to greet Lily.

"Wow, so proper," the blonde girl said with her arms and legs crossed, "—And I'm Esther." Gabriel reached out to shake Esther's hand.

"Would you prefer like, a high five or something?" he asked.

"I was just kidding—handshakes are cool... I guess," Esther chuckled.

"Yeah—the coolest."

The three of them sat silently for a moment. Lily looked down at her shoes, while Gabriel kept smiling at her. Esther took a sip out of her beverage and squinted her eyes at Gabriel. Conversation got quiet really fast and Gabriel hid his face in his arm by scratching the top of his head. With his eyes he motioned for Gustavo to interfere.

"Gabriel!" Gustavo shouted.

"Yeah w-what's up?" Gabriel replied immediately. Gustavo walked over to their table.

"So... did you finish that homework you had?" Lily leaned in to hear Gabriel's response. Gabriel had an open mouth, but no words. "Bro, come on," Gustavo complained sarcastically.

"It's all good, I have until Friday."

"Oh my gosh! I'm the same," Esther butted in with her overly hyper voice, "I won't do whatever until like—the last day."

"You so do," Lily cracked up.

"Nah—I'm not like that at all," Gabriel denied.

"Are you kidding? All the time," Gustavo corrected. Lily and Esther laughed at Gustavo's remark while Gabriel's face turned red.

"Whatever, no I don't. Just... recently maybe," Gabriel said.

"Bro-ho-ho," Gustavo laughed mockingly as he walked away to help a customer.

"So… Um—forget everything you just heard." Gabriel widened his eyes. "Lily, how is your face?"

"It's okay, but I feel a bruise coming on," Lily replied. Gabriel let out an acknowledging, "Mhmm," before taking another sip of his coffee. By habit, Gabriel filled his cheeks full of coffee like a chipmunk and washed it side to side. Esther looked at the both of them like there was something she knew that they didn't. There was, without a doubt, tension, but it was a good kind of tension.

"Oh my gosh, you two are so weird," Esther commented. Gabriel choked on his drink. He pointed his finger at Esther while trying to stop coughing. "I think you're the only weird one right now."

"What? No, I'm not."

"Mm-ya-huh," Gabriel shook his head yes.

Lily laughed yet another time. At this point Gabriel noticed how Lily had smiled or laughed at every one of his remarks and quirky facial expressions. He didn't know why she did, but it definitely wasn't because his jokes were any good. In this time all he could think of was how great it felt to make Lily smile. No doubt there was chemistry between the two, or so Gabriel assumed.

"Well, I still have some homework left," Esther said, breaking the silence.

"Yeah, I need to get going too," Lily added. An almost too quiet to notice, "No," came out of Gabriel's mouth. He noticed Lily's eyes shift slightly in his direction.

"Uh, yeah, me too actually. I have somewhere to be," Gabriel got up with them, holding onto the hope that Lily hadn't heard his silent, "no."

"Hey, could you maybe—" Lily began asking.

"Walk you to your car?" Gabriel filled in.

"I don't quite yet have a car, but you could walk me to the bus station—maybe?" Gabriel wanted to offer Lily a ride, but didn't want to come on strong.

"To the station? Yeah—psh! No problem."

"Cool," Lily said, her smile too cute to say no to. Esther bit her lip at Lily and raised her eyebrows suggesting she wasn't fond of Lily's idea.

"Yeah, cool uh—Let me help you with that," Gabriel grabbed Lily's coat.

"It's fine, I got it," Lily said, softly taking the coat from his hand. Esther hugged Lily.

"I'll see you tomorrow, Lil's."

"Bye boo," Lily hugged Esther back, and Esther promptly left.

Gabriel and Lily walked a large portion of the way to the station in silence. They observed the trees around them like it was their first time seeing trees. The parking lots around them were vacant, a soft wind chilled their lips, and the far away city noise dissipated into the crisp air.

"Would you like my number?" Lily asked spontaneously.

"That would be awesome actually!" Gabriel responded with a glowing smile. He slowed down his pace and patted his pockets, "I don't know where my phone is."

"That's okay, it would be a boring way to give you my number anyway," Lily chuckled, "Do you have something to write with?"

Gabriel happily swung his bag off his shoulder to get a pen. He swung the bag a bit too fast and few of its contents flew out, including his black art journal. Gabriel stooped down to pick up what fell out, reaching for his art journal first. He noticed how Lily pretended not to see him reach for the art journal first. She helped pick up a few papers that were scattered and handed them to Gabriel.

"Thanks," Gabriel said, red-faced and embarrassed. He put his bag back over his shoulder and took two steps forward before stopping. He turned back to Lily who didn't move from her place.

"What?" Gabriel asked. Lily kept holding her smile silently. "What? Why are you looking at me like that?"

"You forgot to get a pen out, silly," Lily bit her bottom lip.

"Gah—I'm sorry. I'm a dork sometimes," Gabriel took his bag off carefully to retrieve a pen. Lily wrote her phone number on her café receipt. Her hand briefly made contact with Gabriel's as she handed her receipt. When the two of them arrived at the bus station, the bus Lily needed to board was already waiting.

"That's me," Lily pointed to her bus.

"Okay. I guess this is goodnight—homie," Gabriel said.

"You too."

They lingered for a moment; their eyes were looking at everything but each other. "Okay, goodnight," Lily turned around quickly and walked to her bus. Gabriel remained there until the bus had taken off, holding the receipt with Lily's number on it like it were the last cookie on Earth. He would have called her right then and there if he'd have his phone on him, not even knowing what he'd say. Gabriel embraced the moment with silence. The distant sirens became melodies, the highway became an orchestra, and the brakes on the buses became percussions. The music filled his heart, and for a moment he could almost feel his mother smile down on him. It was a freedom Gabriel felt warm in. It felt like he belonged there. It felt like home.

A half an hour after eight, Gabriel drove up to the gas station where he was supposed to meet Blake and Noah.

"Hey, buddy!" Blake shouted as Gabriel got out his car.

Blake had long dark hair that curled around his albino ears. He had a flower tattoo on his right arm and two shining studs pierced through his ears.

"What's up bro!" Gabriel hugged Blake, "Man, you were right, this place smells."

"Dude! We called and called—Where the heck have you been?" Noah grumbled.

"Sorry, I didn't have my phone on me," Gabriel replied as he hugged Noah.

"Yo, are you coming to help me move on Friday?" Noah asked Gabriel.

"Oh man, I've got school all day."

"All day?" Noah asked.

"Yeah, I've been having a hard time with my stupid English stuff and my teacher wants to meet at the Library."

"Oh English stuff, huh?" Noah gushed, "I can tell you're having trouble since you call it, 'English stuff.'"

"Leave the poor man alone," Blake butted in, his over-expressive tone made it obvious he was buzzed.

"I'm just saying," Noah responded.

"No, you're just tipsy." Blake turned to Gabriel and continued, "He had an eventful day, just look at him."

"Aha—what gave it away?" Gabriel asked.

"Your eyes man, they're tired."

"Nah—I'm not tired—just… met someone," Gabriel said with a smirk.
Both Noah and Blake became totally quiet, watching Gabriel with undivided attention. "What?" Gabriel asked.

"She better be hot," Blake bumped Gabriel's elbow like a good bro.

"Pft—You should see her," Gabriel puffed, "She's a ten."

"What's her name?" Noah asked

"Lily."

"Like the flower?"

"Yep, like the flower." Gabriel nodded yes.

"Well, did you get her number?" Blake asked. Gabriel threw the most confident look he could muster up at Blake, despite knowing he probably wouldn't have had Lily's number if she hadn't offered to give it herself. "My boy!" Blake exclaimed, his nasty alcohol breath swept across Gabriel's face.

"Just be careful," Noah voiced his concern.

"I got this bro, don't even worry," Gabriel reassured, "Anyway, we're here to celebrate Blake." Gabriel put his hand on Blake's shoulder. "I wish you didn't have to leave, and I'll miss you tons."

"Yeah buddy!" Blake raised his beer bottle in the air.

"That's probably what I'll miss the most," Gabriel said, "Hearing you say 'yeah buddy' all the time."

"Then come to Portland," Blake suggested, "I know you've got school, but like, whenever you're done with that you should come through."

"I'll keep that in mind. I probably wouldn't move there, but visit for sure," Gabriel said.

"Yeah, me either," Noah added, "By the way... I prepared a mini speech."

"Ah—no way! Let's hear it," Blake exclaimed.

Noah got his phone from his pocket and cleared his throat.

"Okay so—here it goes... 'Hey bro, wish you didn't have to leave tonight. I still don't fully get what you're doing there, or how you're even getting there without your own car, but I hope you have a safe trip and a good time. Portland better be good to you, or else I'll have to kick its butt,'" Noah read.

"Thanks buddy," Blake said.

"You know I've got your back," Noah hugged Blake, "And you too, Gabe."

"Me too," Gabriel responded, "We all got each other's back."

The three of them hugged each other and held their pose for a few seconds. Gabriel looked at Noah with a squint in his eye.

"Yeah buddy," Blake whispered.

"Ay!" Gabriel and Noah shouted in unison. "There it is!"

"We were wondering how long it'd take for you to say that," Noah said.

"What? Why you guys always gotta pick on the little guy?' Blake chuckled.

"Because you literally always say that," Noah snickered.

"Yeah whateve's," Blake said dismissively, "Hey, by the way—you should go get some drinks"

"I'm not sure if that's a good idea," Noah said.

"Just get some, I wanna have a good time before I leave."

"Can you guys just be over twenty-one already so I don't have to get stuff illegally," Noah said as he turned and jogged towards the mini mart.

"I'm gonna miss you a lot, bro," Gabriel told Blake.

"Me too, man. Me too."

When Gabriel got home that night, he opened his art journal and watched that dot in the center of the page as he searched his heart for an emotion to express. Although there was usually an emptiness of mind that would follow whenever he opened that journal, this time there was Lily. He knew it would be better to focus on his schoolwork, or any of the other things going on in his life, but Lily consumed his mind that moment. He wondered what his mother would advise; if she'd tell him to get his priorities straight, or maybe she'd encourage a relationship. It was a gamble, but it was a gamble he was ready to take.

Chapter 3

S am groaned, "Dad, you've got too many things to stress over today—Gabriel really shouldn't be one of them."

"We call ourselves a family business for a reason," Leon said as he sat down at the kitchen counter and picked up an Urban Post street-paper to read.

"What the heck is he going to do?" Sam complained, raising his hands up in question, "What can he possibly do for the company?"

"You're missing the point, Sam."

"I'm missing the point? Let me ask you this—say we hire him, and he can't handle it. Next thing you know he will want to quit and go back to college to study whatever the heck he is studying—Then what?" Sam ranted. Leon clinched his eyebrows together and took a sip of coffee. "—Gabriel's not even passing his classes. How are you going to put him in management?" Sam continued.

"Listen," Leon calmly said, taking off his glasses and setting down the paper, "Gabriel isn't like you. He was never as professional as you. If we don't hire him now, it's possible that he may never find a stable job."

"I don't care where he works, just not for me," Sam stated vehemently.

"Then it's a good thing you're not in charge."

"Dad."

"Sam!" Leon raised his voice, "I—not you, but I— am going to do this for him. I'll start him off easy. I'm sure we can find him a task that he can handle."

"I disagree," Sam grumbled.

"Then what would you have him do, Sam?"

"I honestly don't even know," Sam said, "He's better off selling himself on the street."

"You're giving me a job?" Gabriel asked quietly from behind the corner, interrupting the discussion. Leon and Sam both looked at Gabriel like he was a ghost.

"Yes, Gabriel. We are changing some things around with the paper and it'll provide you with a chance to finally have some work," Leon said.

"It's a job, man—A real job," Sam added, "You should be thanking dad,"

"I know that, it's just that I'm a little thrown off," Gabriel said, looking at the floor, "You do know I still have this semester to finish, and then another?"

"That college isn't for you. You aren't learning anything there." Leon stood up from his seat.

"Just because you dropped out of high school and were still able to make a good living, you think school is a waste of time for everyone," Gabriel snapped.

"Your teacher, Brian, told me you want to study Aerospace physics next," Leon piped in, his face became more and more red, "What will you do with that?"

"So what?" Gabriel shouted, "Why do you have a problem with what I want to do?"

"I have a problem because I know all you're doing is trying to kill time so you don't have to work."

"That's a load of b-s," Gabriel grumbled, "You know, you're so full of it—Mom was nothing like you."

"Get over your childhood drama," Sam interjected. Gabriel was aggravated at the mere tone of Sam's voice.

"You—can just shut up!" Gabriel pointed his finger at Sam's face.

"You get all pissy so easily," Sam snickered, smacking Gabriel's hand away.

"Oh, and you don't?"

"That is exactly what I'm talking about. I should get you a behavior counselor, or maybe just a baby-sitter," Sam jeered.

"And that's what I'm talking about," Gabriel shot back, "You expect me to be an adult but then you treat me like some kid. That's your problem."

The temperature of the room seemed to rise as the mutual hostility increased. Leaving his coffee on the counter, Sam started approaching Gabriel rather aggressively. Gabriel wasn't going to back down; he clenched his fists at Sam in protest.

"Look at yourself! This isn't middle school," Sam pointed out Gabriel's defensive pose.

"Stop saying that!" Gabriel roared, "Make up your mind—you want me to be grown up? Then you should treat me that way."

"You want to handle this like a grown up, huh?" Sam began folding his sleeve back, maintaining deep eye contact with Gabriel. Gabriel toned down and stepped back and to the side.

"Hey... look," Gabriel said.

"What? You said you want to handle this like an adult. So come on!" Sam barked.

"No look." Gabriel pointed. "—Dad's on the floor."

Sam turned around and froze for a moment.

"Oh my god, Dad!" Sam Rushed to Leon. Gabriel stood motionless, trying to assess what was happening. Sam got his phone out and called 9-1-1.

"Hello? Yes—my dad passed out on the floor, we need someone to come asap!" Sam yelled into the phone. "He's the owner of Urban Post street paper and—What? Uh... I don't remember our—" Sam moved the phone away from his face. "What's our address?" He asked Gabriel. Gabriel continued to glare at Leon, petrified. "Address!" Sam shouted.

"I— "

"What's our address?" Sam repeated.

"I don't know!" Gabriel's voice cracked.

"Then go to the office and find an envelope with our address on it!" Sam shouted before getting back on the phone. "—Hello? Are you still th—yes I'm not sure what happened but he passed out randomly and his head is all sweaty and—" Sam began speaking into the phone until he looked at Gabriel again, "Why are you still standing? Go!"

Gabriel panicked and darted out of the house instead of into the office; getting straight into his car and speeding away. His hands shook, and lip quivered as he drove directly to college. He arrived on campus, still caught up by the image of Leon on the floor, and waited a few moments in his car. He grasped the steering wheel firmly and looking straight ahead while breathing heavily. Like awaking from a dream and immediately forgetting what happened, Gabriel could not recall his drive to school. Everything in the world seemed to be in slow motion except the thoughts in his mind that raced wildly. He speed-walked to the classroom and observed a note on the door that read: *"Class is at the courtyard."* Much too emotionally drained to do anything else, Gabriel plopped to the ground and hugged his knees. He felt physical pain in his throat as he replayed the scene of Leon lying on the ground unresponsive in his mind.

"Wake up," Brian uttered. Gabriel picked his head up only to see Brian looking down along with some of the classmates. "I'm a little disappointed with you," Brian said while unlocking the classroom, "You show up when class is over—and this isn't the first time—you fall asleep right in front of my class, and you show no effort at all, ever." Gabriel eased his head back down, ignoring the students chattering and Brian's lecture. "Look, I won't allow you to sit in front of my classroom. Either get inside or leave," Brian posed, "However, I'd prefer you leave."

Gabriel, angry, dashed off right away.

"Hello?" Lily answered Gabriel's phone call.

"Is this Lily?" Gabriel asked with a shaky voice.

"Yes, that's me. Whom am I speaking with?"

"Lily—It's me, Gabriel."

"Gabriel, Hi," Lily said, "Everything okay? You sound upset."

"Can you meet me?" Gabriel asked.

"What's this about?"

"I'll be at the cafe where we met. If you can't come, that's okay," Gabriel said, "I'm just—I'm so lost right now."

"What do you mean you're lost? What happened?" Lily asked, listening attentively until Gabriel hung up. He hurried off to the cafe. The anxiousness of seeing Lily again made him feel unusually excited. Although the trembling was still there after what happened to Leon, he had a cheerfulness inside that he didn't want to lose. Admittedly, even he was surprised with himself how fast his mood was able to change.

Gabriel approached Gustavo first thing upon entering the cafe.

"I need your help," Gabriel stressed, placing both hands on the counter and taking heavy breathes.

"And hello to you too," Gustavo replied.

"Oh, yeah—hi," Gabriel laughed nervously, "Sorry, I'm just excited—there's this girl coming here soon."

"A girl?" Gustavo lifted his brow.

"Her name's Lily," Gabriel smiled, "Like the flower."

"Do you need help getting rid of her?"

"What? No—no, nothing like that. Okay, so this girl is about to show up, at least I think she is, and I need you to play some mood-setting music when she gets here," Gabriel babbled, "I don't know for sure if she is actually gonna come, but I think I convinced her well enough to come. Anyway, I was thinking—"

"Bro," Gustavo interrupted "My shift is over."

"Ah come on! Don't tell me that annoying Nathan-dude works next," Gabriel said, "The one who always calls me Gabey-baby?"

"No—I was just planning to close the cafe early today."

"Could you at least stay here until she shows up—if she shows up?"

"Bro, I can't. Look man, I just want you to know that I worry about you, and I don't want to see you waste your time," Gustavo said.

"What do you mean?" Gabriel asked.

"Your teacher, he comes around sometimes and you know what, I'm just going to tell you that he told me about how you've been having trouble in school—and bro—I just really don't want to see you waste your time on something that isn't a priority, you know?" Gabriel stroked his hair and looked at his feet. "She is just a girl but this is your school," Gustavo continued.

"No, I get it," Gabriel assured calmly, "To be honest with you, I don't think I'll be in school much longer because my dad doesn't want me going anymore." Gabriel's eyes became lost the very moment he mentioned his dad, "Which by the way my dad, uh—I don't know what happened, but I think he went to the hospital."

"The hospital?" Gustavo voiced his concern, "What happened?"

"Like I said, I don't know what happened, but he passed out and then I came straight here."

"That's not good bro," Gustavo dropped what he was doing and leaned closer to Gabriel.

"I know, but he told me he wants me to quit school because he thinks I should find a job already."

"I'm sure he will be okay bro." Gustavo became distracted. Gabriel noticed Gustavo looking past him and turned around only to see Lily walking up to the cafe. His heart beat out of rhythm as soon as he saw her. She stayed by the door with her bag around her shoulders, wearing a dark sweater with a rose on it. Gabriel's behavior rapidly changed back to how it was before. He rushed out the door.

"Lily," Gabriel spoke softly.

"So… what's going on?" Lily asked.

"A lot, actually. Can we go for a walk and talk about it?" Gabriel asked. Lily's posture suggested she felt extremely uncomfortable, but she motioned with her head to get started on the walk. Gabriel wasn't happy with how awkward Lily seemed to be feeling so he tried to ease the tension by saying, "I just want to say thanks for coming."

"Is that all you want to say?" Lily responded sternly, but not condescendingly.

"And I guess I'm also sorry for hanging up on you," Gabriel mumbled.

"It's fine, but I don't like those sort of phone calls. So tell me what's going on, because I'm very confused."

"Okay... gosh—I just got really low, you know?" Gabriel sighed as he began explaining, "I'll just start from the beginning I guess. So my brother Sam hates me, right, and this morning I heard him and my dad talking about me. They were saying stuff like I should quit school and come work for the company that my dad owns, but Sam was against it because he's never liked me," Gabriel continued, kicking the pebbles on the sidewalk as he talked "I don't know, I'm still in school and I guess I just don't really want to work alongside homeless people."

"Homeless people? What sort of company does your dad have?" Lily asked.

"Well, I'll just explain it the we my dad would. It's called 'Urban Post' street-paper, and so basically it employs homeless and low-income individuals by giving them this paper—they go and sell it on the street for a dollar a piece, and when they need more they get it from my dad for twenty cents per copy."

"Ah, cool! So wait, why do they have to pay for it?" Lily asked.

"Well, when they sign up, they get a certain amount of papers for free and they usually end up making a good amount of money off it. All they need is an ID to sign up, and it's cool because a lot of these people that sign up have medical conditions that prevent them from getting real jobs, or some people have bad records and so they can't find jobs anywhere else," Gabriel continued to explain, "Anyway, whenever they sell all of their first papers, they come back and get more at twenty cents per copy, then again, they flip it on the street and keep the profits and donations."

"Wow, I'm a bit intrigued actually. What is in the paper?"

"It's all written by the vendors that sell it. It basically has a lot of stories of what homelessness is like and stuff."

"Aw—That's really neat that your dad does that for them."

"Yeah, it is!" Gabriel shouted unexpectedly, "He helps a lot of people."

"You're so weird," Lily cracked up.

"Your face is weird," Gabriel mocked playfully.

"Well, I'm sorry," Lily replied, "—It's the only face I've got."

"Really? I've got a whole bunch back home," Gabriel said, pointing behind himself with his thumb.

"Oh yeah?"

"Yeah, I have a bag of 'em! A bag of faces—that's... never mind. That sounds really scary," Gabriel jeered.

"Sorry for interrupting, but you should keep telling me about your morning," Lily said.

"Oh yeah—what was the last thing I said?" Gabriel asked.

"You were crying about how your brother Sam is so mean to you," Lily teased.

"No, but he is, though!" Gabriel complained, his voice no longer jolly, "Sam's always been a jerk to me."

"How come?"

"Because Dad always liked him more than me, so he thinks it's okay to treat me like crap."

"You don't know that."

"No, it's true, I've always been closer to my mom because of that."

"Aw, mama's boy," Lily cheered.

"Sam works with my dad so they get to spend more time together. Dad's more about business and serious stuff—my mom's actually the one who taught me how to ride a bike, not dad."

"Hmm, have you told your mom how you feel?" Lily asked.

"No, never really did," Gabriel replied, "And you should know something about her—she passed away three years ago."

"Oh—I'm so sorry," Lily said, gently touching Gabriel's forearm.

"It's okay."

"Ugh… I feel so bad now."

Gabriel marveled at Lily's innocent spirit; her way calmed him.

"Don't feel bad. I didn't mention it to make you feel bad."

"Still," Lily said, "I'm sorry for reminding you about it."

"Nah, don't be," Gabriel smiled, "I'm okay, really."

Time seemed non-existent for Gabriel. He had hardly noticed they had already walked far from campus, onto a trail that led to a pond in the woods. The gloomy sky reflected off of the perfectly still water, setting a scene of utter serenity. Something about making Lily smile and feeling the heat radiate off her shoulders set Gabriel's heart ablaze, causing him to slowly melt away with every moment they shared. He knew so little about her, but what he felt inside was too real to ignore.

"Well this place is pretty," Lily commented, leaning on a wooden rail on the dock. Gabriel sniffed, and turned his head to Lily slowly.

"You're pretty," He said.

"Ha—not really," Lily replied, holding her smile so contently.

"What?" Gabriel exclaimed as his eyes broadened, "Are you joking—You've got to be joking because you look amazing!"

"I appreciate that, I really do but," Lily said, her smile reduced half in size, "I just don't feel that way."

"Well I'm perplexed," Gabriel boldly stated, "How can that even be possible?"

"Whoa, 'perplexed!'" Lily chuckled, "Some big words you're using there."

"No but it's true!"

Lily snorted from laughter, blushing and shyly looking at Gabriel's feet.

"I mean look at you!" Gabriel motioned his hands at Lily. "You should be the queen of Egypt with that kind of beauty."

"You don't have to say all that," Lily replied, "Thanks though, really."

"You're freaking welcome," Gabriel kicked his foot behind the other and took a quick bow. Lily giggled again. It was difficult for Gabriel to understand what was going on in Lily's mind. She had a strange look on her face like she wasn't sure of something. He figured she was still thinking of how she didn't feel pretty. Despite how Lily may have felt about herself at the time, Gabriel was willing to spend every minute necessary to make her believe that she was beautiful.

"Hey, we should probably go," Lily suggested.

"Alright," Gabriel agreed, "Come on, I'll walk you to your car."

"I don't have a car. You keep forgetting."

"Ah, bus station then?"

"Sure, I'd appreciate that very much."

"Actually… I could drive you home if you want," Gabriel nervously suggested.

Lily thought about Gabriel's offer for a few seconds before replying, "That's okay, the bus is perfectly fine."

"Cool, uh—is there any particular reason why you don't have a car?" Gabriel asked.

"None of your business, you dork," Lily said, teasingly punching Gabriel's stomach.

"What? I'm just asking," Gabriel humored, "By the way, what are you doing tomorrow?"

"Well," Lily dragged her voice, "I have a job interview in the afternoon, and then I was just gonna stay downtown until seven for a friend's birthday."

"That's like—"

"Like seven hours," Lily filled in, "I know."

"What are you gonna do for seven hours?" Gabriel asked curiously.

"I don't really know yet," Lily shrugged, "I'm pretty good at finding things to do by myself though."

They came to a stop at a street curb. Although Gabriel didn't like the idea of Lily being by herself for such a long period of time downtown, he saw it as the perfect opportunity to meet Lily again and keep her safe from the downtown thugs, should there be any. Gabriel made up his mind, he was going to surprise Lily after her interview. Lily looked at the vacant roadway and began to cross it while Gabriel remained on the sidewalk.

"Come on, doofus," Lily called out, "Are you afraid of jaywalking?" Lily teased.

"I'm not a very 'law-breaking' kind of person," Gabriel said as he cautiously took a step out into the street.

"Wait, are you really afraid of jaywalking?" Lily asked, "Like, actually?"

"It's not that I'm scared—I'm just." Gabriel looked both ways and then sprinted across the street like he was a mouse escaping a predator. "—I'm just not trying to get caught doing anything illegal," he finished when he reached Lily.

"It's just crossing the street. I don't think you'd get locked up for it," Lily stated.

"I know, I'm just saying because my dad would be like… super mad," Gabriel said. Lily's grin suggested she was in disbelief of anything he was telling her. "Alright, I'm scared to jaywalk—sheesh!" Gabriel admitted, "I just really hate doing illegal stuff. It makes me freak out."

"That's adorable, actually." Lily grinned.

They reached the bus station. Gabriel was satisfied at how smoothly conversation seemed to flow. He couldn't deny he was developing strong feelings for Lily. Although he had always been careful about those whom he allowed too close into his life, this time he didn't even put up a fight. Tomorrow couldn't come sooner. As he waved farewell to Lily, she blew a kiss back. That gesture was all it took to melt Gabriel's heart. That very night, he went to sleep with Lily in mind, and in doing so, Gabriel fell for Lily like the very rain that fell when they met, deluged.

Chapter 4

Gabriel woke up with a spirited smile on his face and a joy in his heart. Typically, he wasn't fully awake until he had his fix of morning coffee. Even simpler tasks like brushing teeth would be a struggle, but this morning was far different than most. Today Gabriel planned to surprise Lily downtown. Although she wouldn't be finished with her interview until after-noon, he couldn't wait a moment longer at home. He hopped out of bed and into his car, and rushed downtown.

Most of the duration, Gabriel mulled over different ideas to himself on how he could surprise Lily. Whether it was to call her as soon as he arrived downtown, or to wait until she would leave her interview, Gabriel knew that he wanted to show maximum effort. Sure enough, the moment he saw the vastness of Seattle's downtown right before his windshield, he knew exactly what he wanted to do. He texted Lily,

Gabriel: *Hey when do you get done with your interview??*

Lily didn't respond right away, so Gabriel continued into downtown. He found his way to the market where the vendors were peddling their goods. After exploring all the intriguing jewels and pretty peonies in the market for an extended amount of time, Gabriel came to rest on a sidewalk. He waited patiently until noon, when Lily finally replied. He was anxious, hoping she wouldn't say anything that would cancel his plan.

Lily: *I'm already finished up and I'm just going to get food.* *:)*

Gabriel: *Sweets! Okay so I'm going to text you something and you just gotta trust me and do as I say.*

Gabriel scurried away from the sidewalk, trying not to draw too much attention to himself, lest Lily spot him, and went to the first spot he could think of, "The gum wall."

Gabriel: *Step 1, go to the gum wall. Step 2 locate the pink heart that has 'J + T' inside of it.*

Lily: *Okay... what's this about?*

Gabriel: *It's about you! Now just follow those two steps and then await further instructions.*

Gabriel patiently waited behind a set of stairs, spying through a small window that overlooked the gum wall.

Lily: *Alrighty I found it! What's next?*

Gabriel: *Face the heart and take two steps to the left.*

Gabriel giggled childishly as he watched how clueless Lily appeared.

Lily: *Done... What's the point of all this?*

Gabriel: *The point is that I want you to turn around now and try to spot a little window. It should be right in front of you and a little up.*

Lily turned around and for a moment could not spot the window Gabriel was talking about. Her clueless expression was too funny for Gabriel to watch. He bent down to be out of sight and held back his laughter as best he could. Gabriel felt his phone vibrate from Lily's continued texts. It wasn't even worth reading them at this point. Gabriel took a deep breath and popped his head out the window once again. He could see Lily glaring down at her phone. Worried that Lily might leave, Gabriel knocked on the glass to get her attention. Immediately Lily looked up, only to find half of Gabriel's face peeking from the bottom of the window like a meerkat peeping from a burrow. Her face lit up like fireworks. Gabriel rushed down the stairs. "Hi, Lily!" He screamed, greeting her with a graceful hug.

"Gabriel, what in the world are you doing here?" Lily asked, her face stunned.

"I just didn't want you to be alone after your interview," Gabriel said.

"Aw!" Lily gasped, "That just made my day."

"Come on," Gabriel said, pulling Lily after him, "Let's go see the fish market!"

"How did you know everything was going to work out so perfect?" Lily asked.

"I didn't know, I just improvised when I got here."

"This is so sweet Gabriel, seriously."

"I'm glad you think it worked out perfect," Gabriel grinned shyly, "Now come on, I want you to see this place."

"But I've already seen everything around here."

"What do you mean? Did you get here early?" Gabriel paused in his tracks.

"No you goof—I basically live downtown, so I've seen everything already," Lily replied. Gabriel's smile dwindled just a smidge. "—But," Lily added, "We can still go wherever you wanna go. I can see it all again."

"I'll find something you haven't seen yet," Gabriel said, "You just watch."

"Okie dokie, but I gotta warn you that it won't be so easy."

Gabriel accepted Lily's words as a challenge. He spent hours taking Lily places he found interesting, hoping that she would discover something new. Lily teased Gabriel every new spot they visited, saying she had already seen it and that Gabriel should just let her lead instead. Still, he was too determined to give up. They paid no attention to the soreness in their feet as they explored the emerald city of Seattle until the sun began to set. Finally, they arrived at the waterfront, and walked out onto the dock that extended far into the sound.

"So, you should know that I appreciate you keeping me company all day," Lily mentioned.

"The pleasure is all mine, but how about that birthday thingy you were going to go to?" Gabriel asked.

"That was an hour ago."

"I know—I'm sorry if I kept you from it," Gabriel said, "I can take you there right now if you want."

"No, it's fine. I didn't really want to go anyway, and you gave me a reason not to."

Gabriel smiled. He admired the way Lily was able to make him feel special so effortlessly. There was something about her movement, her walk, that reminded Gabriel of his mother. No matter how much he questioned it, he couldn't deny that he was in too deep to let go of Lily now. Just then, he had the idea to tell Lily how he felt about her. He took a deep breath, and before the first words could escape his tongue, Lily pointed past his shoulder.

"That right there!" Lily exclaimed, "I've never been on that Ferris wheel."

Gabriel turned around, frustrated at the Ferris wheel for interrupting—what would have probably been—the most important words he would have ever said.

"I'm sorry, what were you saying?" Lily asked, refocusing her attention to Gabriel.

"You know what—It wasn't even that important," Gabriel said, "Let's go. I'll take you for a ride."

"Are you sure?" Lily gasped.

"Am I sure I want to take you somewhere you haven't been yet? Uh... Let me think—Yes!" Gabriel laughed, "C'mon!"

Seeing the way Lily's eyes lit up like they did when she saw the Ferris wheel meant everything to Gabriel in that moment. The two of them hurried over to the pier and got on. Lily kept rambling on about her excitement, but Gabriel could only rehearse his feelings for her in his head. Once they boarded the attraction, there was no way out for Gabriel. He knew he had to share how he felt now, the hard part was getting around to it.

"So Lily," Gabriel slurred his words. Lily looked at him when his phone unexpectedly vibrated in his pants pocket, but he didn't hesitate to reject the call.

"Who was that?" Lily asked.

"Just my brother," Gabriel grimaced, "So… you know how some people plan out their weddings years before they even have a boyfriend or girlfriend?" Gabriel resumed.

"Yeah sure, like I planned out my wedding already," Lily said.

"Ha—exactly. I planned out my proposal already," Gabriel added, "But anyway— "

"Oh dude, tell me all about it," Lily said excitedly. Gabriel leaned back and took a deep breath.

"Oh, it's gonna be magical," He assured.

"Oh yeah?" Lily leaned forward. "How so?"

"Because firstly, it's gonna take the entire day to do it. I'll start in the morning by surprising her with breakfast and a dress—a very light dress—the kind that waves around in the wind."

"Go on," Lily said, smiling intensely.

"I'll wait for her to eat up, because it's gonna be a long day of course, and then she'll put on the dress. It'll be a dress she feels beautiful in."

"What color?" Lily interrupted. Gabriel took a short moment to think of a good response.

"That will depend on the color of her eyes, I guess."

"That's adorable—keep going. What happens next?"

Gabriel switched seats to sit next to Lily rather than across from her. At this point, they were at the top of the Ferris wheel.

"Well, I'd take her to my car and make her put on a blind fold," Gabriel explained "Then I'd drive to the beach, and there would be a picnic set up. But before any of this, I'd set up a glass bottle to be tied to a rope that was anchored in the water with a note inside it. While she would be enjoying the view of the waves, I'd run to the water and retrieve the bottle and act like it just washed ashore."

"What would the note inside be?" Lily asked, her eyes wider than Gabriel has ever seen,

"At first I thought it should say, 'Will you marry me,' but then I figured why stop there, right?" Gabriel said, "The note would be a treasure map."

"Ah-huh, and where would this map lead?" Lily asked.

"To a boat not far from the picnic. Together we would take the boat across the water to an island or something."

"Is this a tropical place?"

"I haven't got that part figured out yet, but for romance's sake, let's say that it is," Gabriel answered, "Anyway, once we get on the island, there would be horses waiting for us—because what's a romantic proposal without horseback riding on the beach?"

"Right, of course," Lily played along.

"We'd ride the horses down the beach to where the 'x' was marked on the map, except there wouldn't be anything there. All of the sudden— "

"A whale!" Lily shouts.

"What? A wha—" Gabriel chuckled, "Back to the story. So, all of the sudden, a crowd of people would run out from behind the trees and surround us while they cheered our names."

"I still think a whale would be a neat thing to have, but go on," Lily humored.

"Yeah, so this crowd, which would be all our friends and stuff, would surround us while we are still on our horses, and you and I would jump off and— "

"Aw!" Lily interrupted again, this time much louder, "You just said 'you and I.'"

"Oh, I meant like whoever I'm proposing to," Gabriel blushed hardcore.

"Mhmm—sure. Then what?" Lily jested.

"Um, so we'd get off the horses and I'd pick her up and carry her from out of the crowd and up a hill," Gabriel said, his heart was beating so fast that it could physically be heard, "I'd make sure that everyone in the crowd knew to follow us, but eventually let us escape back into privacy. At the top, there would be a garden pagoda with a table of fruit and flowers."

"I don't think a flash mob surrounding horses would be a good idea," Lily commented, "The horses would likely freak out."

50

"Lily, forget the horses. There's a pagoda on a beach!" Gabriel replied.

"Good point."

"To finish I'd have a nice meal prepared and then I'd have a projector screen open up and a video would turn on. The video would be of me asking her dad if I can take his daughter's hand in marriage and then blah, blah, I'd propose."

Gabriel finished explaining and waited for Lily's response. Lily didn't say a word; she just smiled right through Gabriel.

"So yeah, that's how I would propose," Gabriel added.

Lily turned her head to the side, her ecstatic expression was slowly lost.

"Looks like the ride is over," she noted.

Gabriel helped Lily get off the Ferris wheel. Realizing he had gotten too carried away and didn't tell Lily how he felt about her, he began searching for another opportunity to tell her. The moment had to be a good one, and the mood had to be right, he figured.

"Hey, it's getting late," Lily said.

"I can take you home, I brought my car," Gabriel offered.

"Why don't you take me to your college so I can meet up with Esther."

Gabriel was curious why Lily hadn't let him drive her home. He figured it was because she didn't want him to know where she lived. Deciding it would be best to not mention it, Gabriel simply agreed to her terms. He was okay with not knowing, as long as it meant he got to spend more time with her.

When they were not far from campus, Lily said to Gabriel, "Actually, Esther just texted me and she said she isn't there anymore."

"So, what should I do?" Gabriel asked.

"Just pull up to the bus station."

"Yes ma'am."

"Oh gosh that sounds terrible," Lily huffed, "Please don't call me 'ma'am.'"

"You got it—miss whatever-your-last-name is," Gabriel said.

"Is that your way of asking me what my last name is—because, smooth," Lily winked.

"Maybe."

"Ah—well, my last name is subject to change so…" Lily said as she switched between looking at Gabriel's lips and his eyes. Gabriel didn't respond. He was afraid if he opened his mouth, whatever he would say would be completely mood-ruining. They pulled up to the bus station.

"Wait," Gabriel said as he softly placed his hand on Lily's shoulder. He quickly got out of his car and ran around to open the passenger door for her. Then they walked together to the bus without exchanging words. The only sound was the bus' diesel engine idling beside them. Lily hugged Gabriel tightly. Gabriel closed his eyes and embraced Lily back. As he felt Lily's lungs breathing, a memory of his mother came to mind. He knew in his heart there was something about this girl that could bring closure to the loss of his mother.

"Lily, I want to show you something," Gabriel said. He opened his bag and pulled out the sketchbook, handing it to Lily.

"I was wondering when I'd finally get to see this," Lily addressed.

"What do you mean?"

"I saw this when you were asking for my number, it was actually right around here somewhere."

"That's right, I remember," Gabriel nodded, "Take a look."

"Did you make these?" Lily asked as she flipped through the sketchbook.

"Yes," Gabriel replied, "But I wanna show you this last one." He turned to the page that had the dot in the center.

"What's this?"

"I put my pencil right there, and I kept it there until my brother came in my room and told me that mom was dying." Gabriel carefully took the sketchbook back from Lily. "I didn't know what to draw because I knew mom was about to pass away, and without her I was afraid of expressing myself. I realize this now—three years later."

"You seem to express yourself just fine," Lily spoke softly.

"That's just the thing. It's only around you," Gabriel said, taking Lily's hand.

"What are you saying?" Lily asked.

"I'm not afraid of expressing myself around you, Lily."

Lily sighed as she glared deeply into Gabriel's eyes.

"There's nothing wrong with that."

"Yeah but—"

"Look Gabriel, I really need to catch this bus," Lily said before Gabriel could continue. "Thank you so, so much for surprising me and just keeping me company and making me smile—it means a lot to me."

"Yeah, of course," Gabriel said, "Thanks for the incredible day." Lily hugged Gabriel again. Her hair danced like a flame in the wind as she hurried to her bus. Shortly after she boarded the bus, Gabriel came up to Lily's window. He breathed on the window to create a fog. Just as he touched his finger to the window, the cold wind outside dissipated the fog on the window. Noticing this, Lily leaned in and breathed on the same window from the inside of the bus, then put her finger in the same spot Gabriel did. Gabriel moved his finger up and to the right, and Lily followed his pattern. The warmth inside the bus allowed the fog to remain on the window longer than on the outside. He figured there was no better way to share his feelings except to draw it out, which was all he seemed to be good at. The fog stayed just long enough for Gabriel to guide Lily's finger into tracing a heart shape.

Lily lifted her finger off of the window and observed how Gabriel's face fell perfectly inside the heart shape, and she smiled sincerely. The bus started driving, and Gabriel watched Lily peeking through the window all the way until she was out of sight. He remained there with

the sketchbook in his hand, and a heavy beating in his heart. "Yes!" Gabriel screamed at the sky. The cold chills of the Seattle wind and the judgmental eyes of the people around were no bother to him.

Leon was lying in a hospital bed with Sam by his side. Sam called out to Gabriel, but Gabriel remained silent at the entrance of the hospital room, hesitating to walk in.

"So last night, dad had a heart attack," Sam informed.

"Gabriel, son," Leon said, his voice soul-penetrating, yet comforting. Gabriel inched towards Leon, noticing a tear trapped in Leon's eye.

"So what exactly happened?" Gabriel asked.

"My heart… it messed up," Leon said, smiling humbly.

"That's… messed up, dad." Gabriel quoted. He couldn't find the strength to look Leon in the eye for longer than a few seconds.

"I see what you mean when you said he has an odd humor," A female voice spoke behind Gabriel unexpectedly. Gabriel turned around and noticed a nurse smiling back. Her dark hair was much like Lily's, in that it fell straight from her head down to her shoulders where it curled like a waterfall. She had a plump face, and a smile that held a lifetime of joy.

"Mel," Leon said to the lady, "How good that you haven't left yet."

"Of course," Mel responded, "Your heart monitor looks good."

"Never better." Leon kept smiling.

"And you must be Gabriel." Mel nodded. "Your father told me all about you."

"Yep that's me, um—You're his nurse?" Gabriel asked timidly.

"That's correct. Your father, you know, he's a true fighter." Mel focused her attention back on Leon. "He braved through that heart attack like a champ."

"Oh I did all right," Leon blurted. Gabriel had never seen Leon grin so youthfully before. "Sam, Gabe," He continued, "I have something important to tell both of you." He nodded at Mel, and Mel left the room to give them their privacy. "I've decided to sell the house."

"Wait, dad," Gabriel began.

"It's too late already. The house went on the market today, and I'll be staying at Aunt Betty's for the time being." Leon said, "You remember Aunt Betty's house right?" He smiled with moistened eyes. "So many memories there, so many stories." Leon continued, "We still need to talk about your college situation too."

"What's there to talk about?" Gabriel retorted, "Aunt Betty's house is so far from College."

"Shut up, dude," Sam stepped in, "Why is everything always about you?"

"I wasn't even talking to you."

"But I am talking to you."

"Boys," Leon said, his voice raspy and frail, "That's not all," Leon gripped Gabriel by the bottom of his shirt. "—Since you were born, I set aside fifty-thousand dollars every year for both you and you brother."

"That's… a million bucks," Sam quickly calculated, his eyes were lost and wandering.

"Now, there's an inheritance tax of thirty-three percent, which means both of you will have to split the sixty-six percent remaining."

"Thirty-three percent?!" Sam growled.

"Would you chill?" Gabriel spoke in response to Sam, "Why are you so ungrateful?"

"I'm ungrateful that the government is going to take a third of Dad's hard earned money," Sam shot back.

"Boys," Leon said, "This is going to tear you apart. This money is for when you are ready to buy your first homes. With both of you always gone, I figured we don't need a home that's large enough to house three families. You don't know how depressing it can be to walk past those empty rooms—and with your mother gone, I'm just ready for a change."

"Dang Sam." Gabriel leered at Sam. "Dad is trying to help us and all you can think about is the money. You're the nastiest person I've even known."

"Oh so you're totally cool with the government taking three-hundred and thirty-three thousand dollars from dad?"

"I'd rather have the government take that than you get your greedy hands on it."

When Sam heard this he marched around the hospital bed, staring at Gabriel intensely.

"You're gonna call me greedy, when I'm only trying to look out for Dad's money?"

"You're only doing that because you know it's going in your hands!" Gabriel replied, losing control of the volume in his voice.

"You're such a stupid little kid," Sam grunted, poking his fingers at Gabriel's chest, "Maybe you should consider the fact that I was here for Dad all day while you weren't!"

"I was at college!"

"Oh, really? Because that's not what your teacher told Dad."

"What?" Gabriel asked, puzzled.

"Yeah, Brian called dad today. He told us everything, like what you did yesterday. How you fell asleep in front of the classroom and then you ran off like a little coward crying."

"Okay first of all I wasn't sleeping, I was freaking out because Dad passed out on the floor!" Gabriel shouted.

"That's a load of b-s," Sam responded, "If you were so concerned for Dad, you would have been in the hospital with him." Gabriel looked away in shame, puffing his chest. "First you complain that you don't want to work, and you're trying to finish your stupid college classes, but then you go and pull a stunt like this? You're pretty ignorant for saying I'm the nasty person."

"You know what, Sam, I'll tell you—I don't know why you've always hated me, but honestly—screw you!"

"Screw me?" Sam screamed passionately "Screw—me?!"

Leon's heart monitor began beeping rapidly. A squadron of nurses flooded the room. Gabriel saw how Leon began struggling as he breathed heavily and groaned. Gabriel didn't understand why the sudden commotion, but he could sense Sam's rage increasing at the instance. One of the nurses pushed them into the hallway, explaining that there was an emergency and that Leon had to be escorted into a different room. Gabriel ran his fingers through his hair and moaned anxiously.

"This is all your fault!" Sam yelled, his eyes quickly turned bloodshot.

"Obviously this is your fault!" Gabriel shot back. Sam lunged towards Gabriel and shoved him full force. Gabriel crashed into a small table where a stack of pamphlets went flying into the air. He picked himself up and ran away as quickly as his legs allowed him. Anguish overcame him; Tears raced down to his chin and mixed with snot. His whole body tensed up and he repeatedly whispered Sam's name to himself in disgust. The patients and nurses around moved out of Gabriel's way as he speed-walked out into the hospital parking garage. "I hate you,"

Gabriel muttered. He fell against the hood of his car with his back and buried his face into his arm and lowered himself flat onto the asphalt. "Why am I not good enough?" Gabriel questioned, his upper lip curled in disdain. "I've never been good enough."

Embarrassed by all the attention he'd drawn, Gabriel got inside his car and called Noah. Gabriel cursed impatiently between every ring that Noah didn't pick up.

"Hello?" Noah answered.

"I swear I'm gonna kill someone right now," Gabriel growled.

"No you're not, stop."

"Shut up Noah, I'm seriously gonna hurt him."

"You aren't hurting anybody. Just... tone it way down and tell me what happened."

"I'm done, like... with everything. I'm so sick of everything and everyone and—"

"Gabe," Noah interrupted.

"Listen to me!" Gabriel yelled.

"No, you need to listen!" Noah over-shouted Gabriel, "Everyone always has to listen to this and listen to that and blah, blah—nobody loves me—everybody wants me to fail—Dude, stop... being... a baby and grow up."

"No, no, no—I don't need this right now."

"Yes, right now," Noah continued, "You have to learn that it's not all about you."

"I've heard that so many times it's becoming the worst possible thing you could say to me," Gabriel said coldly.

"It's good that you hear that all the time," Noah reasoned, "Every time you complain, it's because you think the world suddenly stopped revolving around you, and you can't help but cry about it."

"You don't—even—know what's going on." Gabriel smacked his hands against the steering wheel. "Like—you should hear me out first."

"You're always feeling so sorry for yourself—and you know what? You've gotten pretty good at throwing pity-parties for yourself. That's really sad, dude."

"No, what's sad is that you can't listen to someone who literally told you he is going to commit murder. Like, I literally said that, and you ignored me."

"Because I know you don't have what it takes to do that."

"Don't dare me."

"Dude, you are not going to kill anyone!" Noah raised his voice, "You're completely missing the point. I get it, you're just mad about something again and— "

"Oh, I'm perfectly on point," Gabriel interrupted, "It's you that isn't on point. You're just mad because Blake and I are better friends than you are, and you know that he is gone so now you think I'm gonna leave, well maybe I will."

"Whoa back up," Noah urged, "Where did that just come from?"

"You're always talking bad about him," Gabriel said, "That's where this is coming from."

"Okay but, we weren't even talking about Blake."

"You've always hated Blake, and now that he left, you think I'm gonna go to Portland and ditch you. That's why you're freaking out on me, and trying to trick me into thinking that I'm the one who is wrong, when really you're the one who is wrong!"

"Alright, you're saying too many things at once, and it's confusing me," Noah said, "First of all, never once did I try to convince you not to leave. I didn't even know you wanted to leave. How about we back-track? How did we even start talking about this?"

"Back track for what? You're just trying to twist my own words against me."

"What the heck, Gabe, I'm being totally serious right now," Noah spoke, agitated, "I don't understand why you're accusing me of all this stuff so randomly—like, we were talking about you first and now suddenly I'm the victim."

"You're the one who was accusing me of feeling sorry for myself."

"Literally everything you're saying is backwards," Noah replied.

"I think you just don't know what you'd do without me."

"I'm perfectly fine without you," Noah clarified, "But yes, I do want you to stay, and you're right, I don't like Blake."

"There—I told you! I knew you hated Blake!" Gabriel exclaimed.

"Only because I found out that Blake did drugs the last time he went to Portland, and you have to admit that he hasn't been the same since."

"Now you're accusing him of being a drug addict?" Gabriel responded.

"Not a drug addict!" Noah shouted, "I just said he tried drugs—Dude, what is your deal?"

"Screw you, Noah. Honestly, screw you and your dumb accusations."

"You are… so salty, my dude."

"And you're stupid."

"I'm stupid? You're calling me stupid? Like… do you realize we're adults?"

"What kind of friend are you if you can't be here for me when I need you?" Gabriel shouted, just before ending the call abruptly.

The realization that there was a large inheritance available fueled the freshly found hope of escaping Seattle, his home. Gabriel had fantasized of executing such a radical feat before, but never had it been so close to being possible. His mind raced, adrenaline coursed through his body, and a numb sensation developed at the tips of his fingers. He was afraid. It was a fear like floating in the deepest end of the ocean, but it was still an idea he wanted to explore.

Chapter 5

"Good morning," Brian greeted Gabriel, who was the first to walk into class, "I'm glad you came early today—well, I'm just glad you came—look, we need to talk about last night." Gabriel walked past Brian without making eye contact. "—Why didn't I see you in class yesterday, or at the Library? Lucy had—"

"My dad had a heart attack," Gabriel spoke up, still avoiding eye contact.

"I'm aware of that," Brian replied, "And I hate to hear about what happened. However, I managed to contact your brother, "Sam" and he told me that your father thought you were in school. He wasn't happy to find out you weren't." Gabriel slowly seated himself at his desk. "—Now, I don't think you understand just how thin the line is that you're walking on, but—"

"My dad had a heart attack," Gabriel repeated, looking into Brian's eyes this time.

"Here is the bottom line," Brian resumed, "As of right now, you're going to fail this class. The only way, and I mean only way, for you to pass is to do that extra credit I gave you, and then show up to class. That's all you need to do—show up. You simply can't afford to miss another day."

"Don't tell me what I can't afford," Gabriel growled.

"What?" Brian responded with a quizzical look on his face. Gabriel's face turned red, his mind was overwhelmed with too many thoughts to count. "—I think you're missing my point big-time. What I'm saying is that you can't afford to miss a single day if you want to pass." Gabriel was unresponsive. Students began to silently populate the classroom.

"Gabriel, are you listening?" Brian asked.

"Don't say my name like that," Gabriel grinded his teeth.

"Okay, I'm fed up with this." Brian came up to Gabriel and got on his knee to whisper privately, "What's the matter with you?".

"You just don't know what's going on in my life," Gabriel said as he put his forehead into his palm.

"Come here," Brian motioned, as he made way out of the classroom. Gabriel jumped out of his seat and strode after Brian. "—Now, tell me what is really happening," Brian asked considerately.

"I just don't need everyone to gang up on me," Gabriel replied, "Like, I feel like I can't even breathe without someone having a problem with me."

"What are you saying?" Brian asked, "Is someone hurting or abusing you?"

"No, nothing like that."

"So you said you feel like everyone is ganging up on you, is this something that's happening at home?"

"No—that's not what I meant," Gabriel corrected, "I'm just sick of not being taken seriously. Like people tell me my problems aren't actual problems, and that I just need to grow up."

"People usually say things like that when they care about you, and not when they are out to get you."

"No, you don't even know."

"You know what, maybe I don't know anything," Brian retorted, "Maybe you're way smarter than me, and I should just shut up. I don't care if that's what you think. As your teacher, my biggest concern is that you pass this class, and that's why I'm going to tell you right now—that you're just gonna have to get through whatever struggles you're going through, and refocus on passing this class."

"I don't have to get through anything!" Gabriel raised his voice.

"You need to stop. I don't have the kind of patience to— "

"I don't care!" Gabriel shouted back.

"Do you have any clue how much effort I have given to see you pass?" Brian questioned, "None of the other students get half the attention you get!"

"Well, don't," Gabriel grumbled, "If you're gonna complain about it."

"I—I can't believe you," Brian gasped, "Just, ignorant and… and childish. Whatever personal problems you're facing—I recommend you find a counselor."

"As if a counselor will do anything."

"Yeah well, 'I don't care,'" Brian spat back, "Get back in class. We're done." Gabriel followed Brian back into the class. He picked up his bag, and immediately headed out of the classroom. Brian had just began welcoming the class when he interrupted himself, "Where do you think you're going?" He asked Gabriel. Gabriel sped up his pace without responding. "Gabriel!" Brian shouted.

"Brian!" Gabriel shouted back mockingly.

"That's it, you're failing," Brian exclaimed, "If you leave, then there's no point in coming back—you'll be finished!"

Gabriel marched to his car. The sheer heat from his forehead was enough to melt a glacier. He questioned why he was still in Seattle, and why he continued to put up with the people in his life. There was only one person worth staying for, and that was Lily. Sitting inside his car, Gabriel dialed Lily's phone number.

"Hello?" Lily answered.

"Hey, Lily," Gabriel responded softly but impatiently.

"Hi," Lily's reaction was cheerful, "What's up?" Gabriel could feel the warm embrace of Lily's smile through the tone of her excitement. He remained silent for a few seconds, just trying to accept the reality of what he was about to ask from Lily. "Hello?" Lily asked. Gabriel took the phone away from his ear; the mere sound of Lily's voice caused him to tremble. "Gabriel, are you still there?

H—hello?" She ended the call. Moments later she returned the call. Gabriel watched the phone ring while a flash-flood of emotions tumbled through him. He continued to let the phone ring until Lily's incoming call ended.

"I have to do this, I'm in too deep now," Gabriel thought. He called Lily back, gripping the phone as he waited to for her answer.

"Hey Gabriel," Lily picked up "I think your phone isn't working."

"Yeah—maybe," Gabriel said, trying not to let his voice crack from being on the verge of tears "So, basically I need to talk to you."

"Okay, why do you sound so suspicious?"

"I need to talk to you... in person."

"Um—well I'm sort of busy, can it wait until later tonight?"

"Not really," Gabriel replied, "Can I come see you now?"

"Sure, I guess," Lily sighed.

"Right now though."

"Yeah I got that. I'm at Esther's house, could you maybe drive here?"

"Yeah, just text me an address."

"Okay, are you sure you can't just tell me over the phone?"

"I wouldn't even know what to tell you right now."

"What's going on with you?" Lily asked, worried as can be, "Did something happen?"

"Can I just see you in person?"

"Yeah, I'll text you the address right now."

"Alright… Thank you."

"Yeah… I'll see you soon," Lily trilled, "Drive safe."

"Yep—see you soon," Gabriel replied before ending the call. He dropped his phone on the passenger seat and stared straight ahead until Lily sent in an address.

Upon arriving at the destination, Gabriel was about to call Lily when he saw her sitting on a playground bench with Esther. Gabriel burst out of his car and hurried to where the girls were seated. Lily noticed Gabriel from a distance, and bumped Esther with her elbow. Esther turned and saw Gabriel too. She quickly got up and left the scene without saying hello to Gabriel.

"Lily!" Gabriel called out. Lily stood up and took a few steps towards Gabriel with her arms open. Gabriel hugged her tightly when he reached her.

"Hey is—is everything okay?" Lily asked, still holding onto Gabriel just as tightly.

"It is now," Gabriel said.

"You had me worried sick."

"I know—sorry about that."

"You better start talking," Lily demanded. Gabriel sat down on the bench and sighed deeply before speaking up, "I don't even know where to start. Why don't you ask me something cause I'm at a loss for words right now?"

"I'm sort of clueless too, so…" Gabriel looked down and kicked his foot against the leaves on the ground. "Talk to me—what's this all about?" Lily asked.

"Lily." Gabriel turned his whole body towards her. "So last night I found out that my dad has an inheritance for me and my brother and… it's a lot of money."

"Okay…" Lily squinted her eyes.

"And so I'm going to move to Portland," Gabriel stated, his focus completely on Lily's reaction, "I've made my mind up."

"When?" Lily asked.

"I mean, as soon as I get the money, I guess," Gabriel replied. Lily's eyes locked onto Gabriel's eyes like magnets.

"Why though?" She asked affectionately.

"The people here," Gabriel replied.

"What's wrong with the people here?"

"It's not really that there's something wrong with the people, it's more about me not fitting in with them."

"I hope you realize the irony in your statement," Lily objected, "People are people, and if you leave to Portland, people there will do you wrong too."

"That's not the point." Gabriel shook his head. "I'm just done with not being wanted."

"Gabriel, that's not true—you are wanted."

"How can you say that when you don't see what goes on at home—how my own family pushes me away," Gabriel nearly whimpered, "All I'm saying is that I'm actually wanted out there."

"That's a little selfish thing to say, don't you think?" Lily asked.

"Maybe it is a little selfish, but what's wrong with doing something good for yourself?" Gabriel reasoned.

"There's nothing wrong with doing something good for yourself but—"

"Exactly, I'm leaving because it's good for me."

"—But it isn't good for you."

"I disagree."

"Okay, whatever—Why are you even telling me this then?"

"B—because… I want you to come with me," Gabriel stated timorously.

"I can't just run away with you, Gabriel."

"I have a lot of money, I can get us a place and we can actually have a life together."

"That's—no." Lily shook her head in disapproval. "I won't even consider that for a second. That's asking way too much."

"Aren't you tired of this place though?" Gabriel argued.

"Not really—no. Not at all actually, and I would never run away with someone I only met three days ago. Do you actually expect me to just drop my whole life and—"

"Lily."

"—And move to Portland?" Lily continued, "Gabriel, this is so ridiculous on so many levels."

"Lily, I love you." Gabriel closed his eyes and grabbed Lily's arm. He felt Lily flinch.

"Gabriel, you need to chill for a moment," Lily said, brushing Gabriel's hand off her arm. "Everything in your life is moving way too fast right now, and I don't know what happened that made you so—flustered? I don't know if that's the right word, but seriously though, you need to just slow down and really think about what you're doing with your life. Specifically, right now."

"I don't care about what's going on anymore, I just care about you," Gabriel said. "I actually don't care about anything else anymore. Just you."

"I, no—I can't do what you're asking me to do."

"Lily— "

"No, Gabriel, that's not how things work," Lily turned around and began walking away, sniffling.

"Wait!" Gabriel shouted. Lily didn't bat an eye; she kept walking, perpetually increasing her speed.

"Lily, wait!" Gabriel shouted again as he ran towards Lily.

"What?" She exclaimed. It was the first time Gabriel heard Lily speak so passionately and loud.

"Do you at least like me back?" Gabriel asked, knowing that whatever Lily would say next had the potential to completely destroy him. He closed his eyes and took the gamble, placing all his faith in Lily's next words. He heard her take a step back, followed by another step, before she replied, "I did yesterday."

Gabriel froze. He opened his eyes and watched Lily walking away in a hurry. The autumn wind whirled her hair around in her black beanie hat. He observed the vacant playground and the leafless trees in the background of where she walked. It was a scene he could relate with; emotionally vacant, and soul buried.

"Please," Gabriel nervously whispered to himself over and over while shaking his head in denial, "Please, please, please no." The music that he heard when Lily was around had faded, and the skin around his eyes darkened. He was tired. Tired of being in constant distress. Tired of always chasing something and never reaching it. Lily helped him cope with his mother's passing, and every word that she spoke traveled right into the deepest wells of his heart. That's why her few words were all the proof he needed to believe that he could be forgotten in a day, even if he left Seattle. Gabriel drove straight to the Hospital.

Mel walked out from inside the room holding a notebook in one hand and a rose in the other. Her rich, dark hair laid flat against her shoulders, matching the color of her matte-black eyeglasses. She was wearing typical blue scrubs with a stethoscope hugging her neck. A natural smile finished her look, though she hadn't yet noticed Gabriel was present.

"Mel?" Gabriel spoke out. Mel was slightly caught off guard when she heard his voice. Her already smiling face lit up more upon recognizing him.

"Gabriel, what a pleasant surprise."

"Is Leon—" Gabriel began asking before Mel comfortably hugged him.

"Leon? He's right inside."

"Oh…" Gabriel said, still uncertain how to react to Mel's touch. "—I'll just go see him then."

"Alrighty sweetie, you take care of your father now," Mel said smiling. She continued down the hall, and Gabriel refocused himself on his mission. He walked up to the hospital room and paused just before entering. The magnitude of this moment sent chills down his spine; he felt like biting off every one of his nails. His thoughts caught up with his heart, and he took his first step inside. Leon was alone in the room, laying in his bed with heart monitors hooked up to different parts of his body. He was already grinning at Gabriel, as if he expected Gabriel to walk in at this exact moment.

"Son," Leon spoke softly.

"Give me the money," Gabriel cut Leon off. There was a spike in Leon's heart monitor at the sound of Gabriel's words. "My inheritance… give it to me."

"Why is your face so red?" Leon asked, a silent cry was evident in his voice.

"Dad, I just," Gabriel gulped, "Please, I just need that check."

"And what are you going to do with it?"

"I'm gonna make my life better."

"What are you saying, Gabriel?" Leon asked. There was something about the way Gabriel heard his name spoken that left a fracture in his soul.

"I'm saying, Dad, there's nothing left for me here," Gabriel explained. He felt like he was staring at a physical manifestation of a memory, except that it wasn't a memory yet, it was happening now. "Dad, I don't have time—I'm leaving," he continued.

"Think about what you're doing. Think about what you're leaving behind," Leon reasoned.

"What? What am I leaving behind—college? You? Everything I'm leaving behind has already left me a long time ago," Gabriel let a tear slip his eye.

"Not everybody left you," Leon reassured.

"Mom did."

"And what would she say? What would leaving fix?"

"Everyone else left me, so now I'm leaving everyone," Gabriel responded, wiping his cheek with his shirt. "I need my money, Dad."

"Seven-four-eight-two," Leon stated with a mellow voice "That's the code to my safe. You'll see two stacks of money, and yours is on the left. Seven-four-eight-two."

Gabriel couldn't stand in that atmosphere any longer. Seeing Leon so helpless, and in one of the most trying times of his life, Gabriel slipped out of the room. Leon called Gabriel's name out with whatever strength was left in him, but Gabriel put his hood on to block out the sound and dodged several nurses as they rushed to Leon's room.

Gabriel drove home, recklessly. The sound of Leon's heart monitor repeatedly resounded through his head. He pulled up to the house and marched full speed into Leon's office, leaving his car idle in the driveway. Sam began calling Gabriel from somewhere inside the house, but Gabriel wasn't able to make out what was said. He punched in the digits into Leon's safe, unlocking it on the first try. Just as Leon told Gabriel, there laid two stacks of money. Gabriel took the left stack.

Sam called out to Gabriel again, his voice was louder this time. Gabriel was far too consumed with the sight of a four-inch thick stack of money. He swiftly sprung around Leon's desk and sprinted back to his car. Sam saw Gabriel escaping in such a rush and ran after him, but Gabriel made it into his car before Sam reached the front door. Sam stepped out, one foot inside the house, one foot on the porch, and again started shouting to Gabriel.

Sam's words were impossible to understand from inside the car, but Gabriel presumed they weren't anything but insults. For the first time, though, Gabriel didn't care what Sam had to say. There was nothing that could be said that would stop him now. He took one last glance at his home through the rearview mirror. Sam was still hurling curses with his fist in the air. The satisfaction Gabriel had experienced from ignoring Sam was too great to not grin about.

Chapter 6

"Here I am. I've made it," Gabriel told himself when he first saw the high-rises of downtown Portland. The lavender sky behind the buildings painted a masterpiece out of the artsy city. It's almost as if the city lights gleamed just for him. The hour was late, and Gabriel remembered he still had to tell Blake about his arrival. He called Blake, anxiously awaiting to hear that familiar voice.

"Gabe! What's up man?" Blake answered.

"Hey bro, how are you?" Gabriel asked.

"Pretty good man, pretty good—What's going on?"

"Well." Gabriel cleared his throat. "I'm uh… in Portland."

"What do you mean?" Blake gasped, "Like… F'real?" He asked.

"Yes, fuh-real," Gabriel answered comically, "Where are you?"

"I'm at a donut shop. Come through, bro!"

"Yep, I'm already downtown, just text me the address."

"Yeah buddy!" Blake screamed emphatically, "I'll shoot you a text right now."

Gabriel was inspirited by Blake's warm welcome. This was the sort of treatment Gabriel had so eagerly longed for. The only challenge was to find what to do with all the newfound freedom he had on his hands, no commitments, and nobody to please but himself. When he pulled up to the donut shop, he saw Blake already standing outside with his arms outstretched, ready to gift the dearest of hugs.

"I could totally go for a donut right now," Gabriel said as he stepped out of his car.

"This is the legit-est place in town," Blake responded.

"You—have—no—idea... just how good it is to finally be here!" Gabriel howled as loud as he could as he greeted Blake with a firm hug.

"You look peckish my friend," Blake said in his best, yet still poor, British accent.

"I hope that means hungry, because you'd be right."

"I think that's what it means—I don't know," Blake shrugged, "Let's go get you some donuts before they close."

As he stepped inside the donut shop, Gabriel noticed a picture of a maple donut topped with bits of bacon.

"Ah heck yeah!" He shouted, feeling high and mighty. The girl behind the counter glared at Gabriel, and even Blake was slightly caught off guard by Gabriel's over-the-top enthusiasm. Inside, there were all sorts of trinkets hanging from the ceiling, and picture frames with no pictures in them on the walls. Gabriel came to the front counter and looked at the girl's thick eye-liner for a few seconds too long.

"Hi, I'm hungry. What would you recommend?" Gabriel spoke up.

"Hi, Hungry—I'm Samantha. Everything we serve is pretty good," the girl replied.

"'Hi, Hungry, I'm Samantha,'" Gabriel repeated her words. "—Aha, you're pretty funny."

"Yeah, okay, what do you want to order?" Samantha said, making her attitude especially evident. With his hands on the counter and body facing forwards, Gabriel turned only his head around and shouted across the room,

"Blake, what do I want?"

"Get the same thing I got!" Blake shouted back. Gabriel returned his attention to Samantha, who was already ringing up the order. He looked up and down Samantha like she was a tasty treat as he handed his debit card to her.

"You're sassy—I dig that," Gabriel mentioned.

"That's great that you think that—please sign this." Samantha handed Gabriel a receipt.

"I usually don't give out my signature for free but… you'll be the exception," Gabriel winked. Samantha couldn't appear less impressed. He dotted his number on the receipt and handed it back to Samantha. "My friends call me Gabriel but… you can call me tonight," He squinted his eyes coquettishly.

"Wow—okay that was cheesy. So, so cheesy," Samantha dragged her words. Blake's chortling was just loud enough for Gabriel to be bothered by it. Gabriel remained by the counter, awkwardly holding the box of donuts that he ordered, and waited for a further response.

"Oh, wait—were you being serious?" Samantha widened her eyes. "Uh... I sort of have a girlfriend."

"A girlfriend?"

"Yeah, one of those—but hey, for a cheese-ball like yourself, you're still somehow sweet," Samantha remarked as she bit her lip and smiled. Gabriel acknowledged her compliment before walking away and sitting down at a booth with Blake.

"That was pretty humiliating," Blake said.

"Yeah, okay," Gabriel denied.

"'But you can call me tonight,'" Blake repeated Gabriel's words mockingly, "Bahaha—what a show."

"If she was straight, she'd totally be into me. I'm telling you."

"Yeah, I'll just let you keep believing that to make you feel better."

"Okay, very funny—ha ha."

"Ah-man, I'm so glad you're back. How long you here for?" Blake asked.

"For good."

"Like... what do you mean, 'for good?'"

"I quit my college and got some money—and so now I'm here," Gabriel said.

"Dude, no kidding."

"Nope—I'm here to stay," Gabriel nodded.

"So that's it, huh?"

"Yeah, that's it," Gabriel leaned on to the edge of his seat to better capture Blake's next reaction. A smile slowly began to appear on Blake's face.

"Yeah, buddy," Blake gushed, "I'll drink to that—er eat a donut."

"Me too buddy—Cheers." Gabriel tapped his donut with Blake's. He couldn't help but snicker from being around Blake. The two of them remained in the donut shop long after dark, engaging in long-overdue conversation. Gabriel wanted to tell Blake about the inheritance money then, but couldn't find the right opportunity. He knew he couldn't leave Blake in the blind forever, but he also knew Blake wouldn't be able to contain himself if he found that the inheritance was over three-hundred thousand dollars.

When the radio ceased to play in the donut shop, Gabriel and Blake knew it was time to leave. They thanked Samantha on their way out and walked to Gabriel's car.

"Hey, where's your car?" Gabriel asked Blake, "Have you gotten one yet?"

"Nah man, you don't need a car when you live in the city," Blake replied. His arms spread open at the whole city.

"Hop in then, mister I-don't-need-a-car," Gabriel humored, "Do you actually live downtown?" He asked as they drove out of the parking lot.

"Yeah—Turn left at the stop," Blake responded.

"So, which dumpster do you live in?"

"Actually I stay with some friends—you'll meet them. They're chill."

"You guys in like an apartment or something?"

"A small office building actually, but we have a whole floor to ourselves."

"Oh, nice, nice."

"Yeah, it's… well, it's not exactly our place," Blake told Gabriel.

"How so?"

"It's actually our boss's place."

"So who do you live with then?" Gabriel asked.

"With Nick."

"W—wait, who is Nick?"

"I live with my friends, but at Nick's place," Blake explained.

"Yeah, but who is Nick?"

"We all share the place that Nick owns. He doesn't stay with us, though."

Gabriel tried to think of the right question to ask to counter Blake's reluctance to answer directly. "Why don't you just meet them?" Blake continued, "Actually—pull up to that curb." He pointed to a vacant parking lot.

The moment Gabriel parked, Blake slipped out like a snake. Gabriel watched as Blake sprinted across the gravel parking lot and into an alley. "What a strange dude," Gabriel muttered. He was used to the fact that Blake had always been the kind of person to escape from uncomfortable situations, but this time it was different. This was a new city, and for Blake to disregard important questions, such as the one Gabriel asked, was not okay in his eyes.

The windows fogged up inside the car. The frigid air crept in from the outside, leaving Gabriel with less and less patience. He checked his phone often, but was disappointed to find texts from everyone except Blake. Gabriel hopped out and trailed over to where Blake had gone, leaving behind his phone in the car. He stood in front of the brick complex where Blake seemingly entered, and scanned the windows to see which room may have been occupied. The cloudy sky stole the moonlight from the city, and Gabriel could not see clearly enough to make out which window had lights on inside. He then looked around the street, only to find fenced off alleyways and vacant residencies. There seemed to be no sign of Blake, or any life, for that matter, and the once glowing city of Portland suddenly felt like a ghost town.

Gabriel called Blake's name out loud, but was treated with silence. The frost developing under his nose wasn't helpful one bit. He returned to his car and phoned Blake, but Blake didn't pick up. With nothing left to do, Gabriel retrieved his sketch journal and stared blankly at it, accepting that he would just have to wait for Blake.

The exuberance inside him evaporated like the very breath he was exhaling. Gabriel whispered to himself, "This hurts more than I thought it would," referring to the emotional ache he felt being away from Lily. "—She's the one that left me, though. I can't do anything to change that." Gabriel grasped his pencil. He knew it would be better to let go of Lily, and give as much space between them as possible, but despite his best efforts, he could not deny that his feelings were perpetually growing. Staying in Portland, or really anywhere else, was the way he decided he would vacate the emotions of his heart.

"Yo!" Blake shouted from across the parking lot. Gabriel quickly folded his journal back into his bag and dashed towards Blake. There were two others that stood beside him, their figures were unrecognizable from a distance. When Gabriel reached the group, he placed both his hands on his knees and panted.

"Hi guys, I'm Gabriel," he managed to introduce himself, still short of breath. A hand stretched forth and Gabriel shook it without looking at who it belonged to.

"I'm Heidi," said the young girl. Gabriel paused his heavy breathing and took a first glance at Heidi, noticing her crimson-red, pixie hair, first. He looked up and down her short body, still holding her shockingly soft hand, before bringing his eyes back up to hers.

"—And I'm Gabriel."

"You already said that," Heidi chuckled. Her coy smile was captivating, and her body equally as alluring.

"Sorry, I just—you—yeah... hi," Gabriel stammered as he let go of her hand.

"Wha-thup, I'm Kit," the Asian-American boy standing beside Heidi said with a heavy lisp.

"Hey bro," Gabriel replied, giving an upwards head nod "So... Heidi."

"That's me," Heidi responded sweetly, her teeth were sparkling like they were on display.

"You look so... decorated," Gabriel motioned up and down Heidi's body and face.

"What's that supposed to mean?" Heidi replied curiously.

"It's just all the colors and bracelets and stuff," Gabriel said. Heidi looked to Blake with an unsettling squint in her eye.

"So..." Blake interjected, "Let's go say hi to everyone else, and then I'll show you around the place," He said, promptly tugging Gabriel's arm. Heidi stooped her eyes to Gabriel's feet and grinned from ear to ear. Several steps later, Gabriel took his gaze off of Heidi and brought himself right up to Blake's ear.

"Did you see how hot she is?" Gabriel whispered loudly. Blake winced in distaste.

"Dude, she is so not."

"I'm serious Blake. Isn't she absolutely gorgeous?" Gabriel continued.

"You really shouldn't go there."

"What do you mean?"

By this time the two of them had crossed the parking lot and came to a black metal door. The door was waist high off of the ground with a set of rustic stairs leading up to it. "What do you mean I shouldn't go there?'" Gabriel persisted.

"Ugh, why do they take so long?" Blake grumbled as he pounded on the door.

"Blake," Gabriel nagged. Just then the large door clanked and opened from the inside. The man inside was holding the door open with one hand, and his phone with the other. Gabriel pegged the man as, what most would call, a metal-head. His long frizzy hair and ghastly band shirt revealed that about him indubitably.

"I'm Auston," the man said while staring at his phone.

"Hey, Auston," Gabriel stretched his fist out. "I'm Gabriel."

"Fist pounds are so funny, dude" Auston remarked as he bumped Gabriel's fist.

"Oh, I do that just because," Gabriel said, "Why are they so funny?"

"They're just so weird, man, you know?" Auston replied with a hushed tone. *"You're the weird one, dude,"* Gabriel thought to himself "Yeah, I guess so."

Gabriel followed Blake up the steps and into the compact, basement-looking room. Not long after, Kit and Heidi joined them. Inside the room was a service elevator that looked like something out of a zombie apocalypse film.

"Ah cool, I've always wanted to ride one of these!" Gabriel exclaimed. Blake lifted up the metal scissor gate on the elevator. There was silence for a good minute after the five of them boarded the lift. Gabriel could not help but notice Auston's almost-sensual smile. Considering there was nothing really interesting going on, Auston appeared just a little too enthusiastic and Gabriel couldn't ignore.

"You smoked out?" Gabriel asked.

"Sure, man," Auston stated, half smiling and half really smiling.

"Aha—Gotchya," Gabriel responded, coming to the conclusion that Auston was probably on something.

"What sort of place is this?" He thought to himself. *"And why are they all dressed like they just came from the best rave ever?"*

Right off the bat there was tension, but not in the way Gabriel hoped it would be. The lift squeaked like the rusty old piece of junk that it was as it began its ascent. To break the silence, Gabriel took a deep breath and asked, "You guys know what the difference is between an elevator and your mom?" He looked down with a smirk, while Blake looked up from his phone and closed his eyes in preparation of a bad joke. Gabriel waited just the right amount of time for the punch line of the joke to reach its maximum potential. "—An elevator can properly raise a child," He finished. Silence was prevalent. Nobody laughed, not Heidi, not Blake, not even Gabriel himself.

"We're all orphans," Auston softly informed; his lively smile was no more. Blake practically slapped himself with the speed of his face-palm.

"All of you?" Gabriel screeched. His heart dropped the moment Heidi turned around.

"Yeah, pretty much." She responded.

"Oh dude—my bad guys," Gabriel pled. He pulled Blake to himself and whispered, "You didn't tell me everyone here is an orphan."

"Wha—how was I supposed to guess you would say something so stupid?" Blake replied irritably.

"I wouldn't have said a 'parent' joke if I knew all of you guys were orphans."

"Maybe you should just not joke at all for the rest of the night," Blake said "—Or like, ever."

Gabriel pulled out his phone and stared at a blank screen as he processed the stupidity of his ignorant joke. When the lift reached the top, both he and Blake waited for everyone to exit.

"That was so dumb. What did you think, like— 'oh yeah I'll just say this garbage joke and Heidi will love me forever,'" Blake mocked.

"I didn't think everyone here was humorless," Gabriel responded.

"Well… there, you said it, you didn't think."

"There's no way Heidi is gonna hook up with me now."

"Oh that's for sure. Actually, if you listen close enough, you could almost hear the lift announce, 'Next stop, the friend zone,'" Blake joked.

The two of them walked to the room where everyone else had gone into. As Gabriel took his first step inside, he was hit with a scent so horrid it could make a grown man weep. Clothes and plastic bags were scattered across the floor, the ramen noodles that were plopped on the floor didn't make the studio-room any more attractive, and a single desk lamp was all that illuminated the space aside from the few windows that were mostly covered.

"This place is a home inspector's worst nightmare," Gabriel whispered to Blake, as he cautiously followed him into the eerie room. "If rats had standards, this place wouldn't even meet them," Gabriel continued.

"Dude, would you just chill for like—ten minutes?" Blake growled, "Just stay behind me and don't talk to anyone."

Gabriel strained his eyes peering into the gloom. In the corner was a clothes rack that seemed too organized to belong in this place. Beside it was a table with something like chemists' gear. A group of teenagers that he had not yet met were huddling around the table like doctors performing surgery. On the floor beside them were several syringes and a splash of what appeared to be blood. Gabriel wasn't sure if investigating would be the wisest of choices, but his curiosity led him to go towards the table.

"So, Nick might be here soon," Blake said, stopping Gabriel in his tracks, "If he shows up I need you to be chill. I'm gonna go to the bathroom first, but you can't stay here right now, so I'll meet you outside. Don't talk to anyone either."

"Hey, I have to tell you something," Gabriel urged.

"Okay—When I get out."

"It's really important."

"We can talk now, but I don't think you'd want to make me stay. Let's just say the turtle is about to peek out its shell."

"Whoa alright, too much information," Gabriel plugged his nose. Blake walked away giggling snottily.

"I'll meet you by the car!" Blake shouted as he walked away.

Gabriel escorted himself outside, trying to not draw any attention. He went back to his car and stared at the money. He felt bad for Blake. The idea that there was nowhere else to stay but a sketchy place like this disgruntled Gabriel.

"What'chya got there?" A voice of an elderly man came from behind Gabriel. Gabriel quickly dropped his bag and shut the car door. He looked at the man speechlessly. The man wore a black leather jacket and a black rose tattoo on his neck. A cold smile revealed his mustard yellow teeth.

"I'm just messing with ya, no need to be so serious," the man humored.

"Hh-yeah, uh…"

"I believe we haven't met. I'm Nick," the man said.

"I'm me—Err… I mean, that's yeah… I'm just… Gabriel." He closed his eyes. "Oh my gosh, what the heck was that?" He scolded himself silently.

"Well, it's a pleasure to meet'chya, kid."
Gabriel got cold feet, and not only because he was standing on the frigid gravel. There was something about the devilish glare in Nick's eyes that intimidated Gabriel.

"I have a question," Gabriel said, "What exactly do you do with them? I mean all the teenagers who live in your apartment."

"Well that's easy to answer. I pick these kids up from the street and give them a place to stay. Most of them ran away from home or never had a home. It's terrible stuff man, terrible stuff, but I try to help," Nick responded.

"If you are just trying to help, why do they live in such a heavily guarded dump?" Gabriel questioned, "— Sorry, that came out kind of rude."

"No worries," Nick replied, "I was an orphan growing up, just like most of kids here. What they do is help me sell CD's in the street. In return, I give them my place to live and a family. It's about all I could afford to give them."

"CD's?"

"That's right."

"What sort of CD's?"

"Well—" Nick began explaining.

"Hey Gabe!" Blake shouted from across the parking lot. Realizing it was Nick that he interrupted, Blake's eyes widened and he shut up.

"Hey Lil' man, where's Pushkin?" Nick shouted to Blake.

Blake stood frozen in place, and pointed over his shoulder to the apartment where everyone else was.

"I gotta take care of something," Nick said to Gabriel. Nick then marched straight to the building like a lioness trailing towards its prey. Blake walked over and met Gabriel half-way in the parking lot.

"You're nickname is Blake?" Gabriel asked.

"Yeah, Nick does that. I don't think I ever heard him call someone by their real name more than once."

"Must be why it's called a 'Nick' name." Gabriel snorted. Blake remained unamused by Gabriel's comment.

"Stay out here," he urged Gabriel as he turned around to walk away.

"Wait up, I need to tell you something." Gabriel tapped Blake's shoulder.

"So do I," Blake looked around impatiently, "But right now is not a good moment."

"Blake, you're starting to piss me off. I have something that I really need to tell you."

"Hold on! I have to tell you what's about to go down," Blake said. Gabriel, on the verge of losing his temper, rolled his eyes and waited for Blake to speak first. "You heard Nick mention 'Pushkin,' right?" Blake asked. Gabriel nodded. "Okay so low-key, Pushkin stole from Nick a while back, and Nick kicked him out because of it, but Pushkin still shows up when Nick isn't around because he makes drugs."

"Drugs?"

"Pushkin cooks crystal, and some of the others help him sell, but Nick isn't exactly cool with it," Blake explained. Gabriel thought for a moment.

"So Nick wasn't supposed to show up, huh?"

"Someone snitched on Pushkin, and if anybody saw that I said he's upstairs, then they are all gonna think that I'm the one who snitched."

"Who actually snitched?" Gabriel asked.

"Heidi," Blake replied, "She told me Pushkin threatened her cause she stopped selling for him, and she was one of his best dealers." Gabriel was beginning to understand the severity of the situation. "Nick is gonna be super pissed at everyone for not telling him about Pushkin," Blake continued. His speech was quieter and quieter with every sentence. "But the worst part is Pushkin. I know him, he is going to figure out who snitched on him and he'll literally kill them."

"Then we got to get outta here," Gabriel said.

"You think it's that simple? Nick doesn't let us have cars or our own money. We have to ask him for stuff if we want it, and he decides if we actually need it or not." Blake said.

"What? Are you kidding me?"

"No—and you need to keep it down. Just let me figure out the situation."

"Why the heck did you want me to come to Portland then, dude? It's like—Hell here."

"Because everything was chill until Heidi snitched," Blake responded.

"Whatever—I can get you out of this," Gabriel said. Blake looked at him dumbfounded. "Follow me," Gabriel motioned to his car.

"What, are we just gonna drive away?" Blake grumbled, "I don't have time. I need to go see what's going on inside."

"Just... Freaking, look!" Gabriel yelled in frustration as he briefly flashed the inheritance money.

"Wait—was that cash?" Blake leaned in.

"That's what I've been trying to show you this whole time," Gabriel said.

"That's like a hundred grand, where did you get that?"

"Shut up," Gabriel whispered angrily as he scanned the surroundings to see if anyone was watching "Nobody can know about this—and, it's more than a hundred."

"Let me see it again," Blake said. Gabriel left his bag ajar. As soon as Blake saw the cash again, he grasped both of Gabriel's shoulders. "Let's get the hell out of here! Let's go to Vegas!" He snapped. His expression was electrifying.

"Vegas?" Gabriel muttered, "I agree with you that we should get out of here, but—"

"And we gotta take Heidi." Blake interrupted.

"I can agree with that, too," Gabriel responded.

"—And Kit and Auston," Blake continued.

"Whoa, wait up—why them?"

"Because they know about Heidi snitching," Blake explained, "Pushkin will find out and he'll literally kill them."

"Okay," Gabriel agreed, "But we gotta go right now."

Just then, something like shattering porcelain resounded from a window several stories up. Shortly after, Heidi screamed. Blake and Gabriel immediately dashed off, leaving the bag behind.

"How are you running so fast?" Blake shouted, huffing and puffing as he sprinted.

"It's a mama-bear instinct," Gabriel shouted back, "—Which is weird because I'm not a bear, or a mama!"

"You always know exactly what to say at the wrong times!"

Blake and Gabriel reached the service lift. Gabriel threw himself against the wall and buried his head in the corner try to catch his breath while Blake called down the service lift. "This is why you came here, man—it's your destiny," Blake said, "You're not the only one who wants to run away."

"No, I want to help you out, and Heidi too, I'm just not sure if I can get the other guys as well," Gabriel said.

"Don't even worry—we're bros—that's what we are, and we're gonna figure this out," Blake reassured.

"Alright man, whatever you say. How do we do this?"

"We take Nick's van and your car," Blake said.

"Are you crazy?"

"Yeah, buddy." A sloppy smile manifested on Blake's face.

"I knew you'd say that," Gabriel shook his head. "Okay, so we just go in and take his keys?"

"Let me handle the keys. You make sure that everyone makes it out," Blake said.

The elevator reached the top floor and the two of them observed how everyone inside stood firmly against the walls. Nick was silent; he stood in the center with a rod in his hand.

"Just—be—ready," Blake whispered to Gabriel.

"Since everyone is here now, why doesn't one of you tell me where Pushkin is, ah?" Nick raged. The room remained silent. "Alright, I'm going to pretend that none of you are mute and ask you one more time—Where is Pushkin?" Nick continued with his verbal onslaught. Blake kept tipping his head towards the exit, signaling that he was making a run for it. Kit, Heidi, and Auston all picked up on it, and they were petrified.

"We've only got one shot," Blake whispered to Gabriel. Nick suddenly turned towards Blake.

"What'd you say?" he asked. Blake nervously avoided eye contact with him. "No, I heard you say something. Why don't you say it again, and a little louder this time?" Nick persisted. Gabriel noticed Nick grip the rod that he was holding a little tighter. Then Gabriel looked at the clothes rack and noticed that the clothes hanging on it weren't as organized as they were when he first saw them. Blake didn't say a word. "Where is Pushkin?" Nick demanded. Blake flinched at Nick's raucous voice.

Nick walked towards Blake and when he was just inches from Blake's nose, Gabriel exclaimed in distress, "He's in the clothes rack!" A shockwave of tension blasted through the room. Nick didn't hesitate, he marched across to the clothes rack. Luckily, it was placed in the corner farthest from the exit. Blake made another round of eye contact with Kit, Heidi, and Auston. When Nick was only a few steps away from the clothes rack, he stopped and turned his body around while his feet were planted. "If you're lying to me Gabriel, boy, I'll kill ya." Nick threatened, just before turning back to the clothes rack. "—Alright Pushkin, you've got nowhere to go."

No sound or movement came from behind the clothes. The silence felt louder than a crowd of sports fans on game day. Everyone in the room was breathing heavily. Nick waited in front of the clothes rack for some time. Each passing second of silence brought Gabriel closer to a nervous breakdown. Nick chucked the rod at the clothes rack, but there was no response. "Are you trying to make a fool out of me?" Nick shouted at Gabriel. The glare on his face was that of a murderer. He began walking towards Gabriel ferociously. Gabriel's hands trembled, and the stress was severe enough to spawn a few gray hairs. "I'll kill ya!" Nick proclaimed. Gabriel, overcome with peril, acted on his nerve.

"Look over there—" he shouted, pointing behind Nick. Gabriel's plea was nothing short of convincing. Nick naively turned around, along with everyone else in the room. Gabriel took the chance; he dashed towards Nick and shoved him with all the might that his lightweight body could muster up. Nick tripped over his own foot and toppled down against the clothes rack. Blake and Gabriel immediately jumped on Nick. Blake battled to hold Nick down while Gabriel rummaged through Nick's pockets.

"The keys are on the swivel!" Blake informed distraughtly. Auston soon joined Blake in the struggle. Everyone in the room began hollering, and Nick's screams weren't of any language on Earth. Gabriel managed to fetch the keys off the swivel that was attached to Nick's belt.

"Let's go, let's go, let's go!" Gabriel shouted as he leaped towards the exit. Blake, Kit, Auston, and Heidi followed suit.

"I got the stick, dude!" Auston yelled as he waved Nick's rod wildly.

"Oh my g—just get in! Hurry!" Gabriel shouted. Kit stumbled over his saggy pants just a few yards away from the lift. Gabriel ran up and helped Kit on his feet.

"Oh my god!" Heidi cried from the top of her lungs.

"We're in like Flynn—hit it!" Gabriel shouted as he stumbled back into the lift.

"Come on, let's go!" Heidi urged.

"It's not working!" Blake's voice cracked.

Nick rounded the corner full speed, bouncing between the narrow hallway walls. Gabriel grabbed Blake's arm and pointed down the hall at Nick.

"Gotta go." He insisted. He then leaped out from the lift and made a sharp turn left to the emergency stairs. Blake and the rest of the squad bolted after Gabriel.

"Oh my god, where do we go?" Heidi panicked. Her paranoia was more miserable than a Chihuahua at a concert.

"Stairs! Over here," Gabriel beckoned.

"I'm gonna kill ya!" Nick hurled his threats from behind.

Gabriel held the door open. As soon as everyone passed through, he stepped through and shut the door. Nick's momentum propelled him directly into the heavy-duty steel door. The collision rumbled the walls of the entire complex.

"Crazy old man!" Gabriel shouted, as he bounced away from the door. The group of runaways dove out the exit door like paratroopers jumping from a plane.

"Go to the van!" Blake yelled. Gabriel was the last of the group to exit the building, running hastily to his car, which was parked directly behind Nick's van. He tossed the van keys to Blake. "Let's dip." Nick was stumbling just a few yards behind him. Blake got into the driver's seat of the van, while Kit, Auston, and Heidi came in through the passenger side. Gabriel got into his car.

"What are you doing?" Blake shouted.

"My car won't start!" Gabriel replied.

"What?"

"I said—my stupid piece-of-junk-of-a-car won't start!" Gabriel turned the key violently and snapped it in half with most of the metal now stuck in the ignition.

"Gabriel, look out!" Heidi screamed out the window, just as Nick came barging in through the driver's side of Gabriel's car.

"I'm gonna kill ya, I swear!" Nick yelled with all his might; his spit sprinkled all over Gabriel. Gabriel immediately grabbed his bag, looping the strap around his hand.

"You're starting to annoy me," Gabriel mumbled as he hopped over to the passenger seat. Nick grabbed Gabriel's ankle with eagle-like grip.

"I'll kill ya dead, boy!" His smoker's breath fanned over Gabriel's face.

"Blake—why do you always lock your door?" Gabriel growled, struggling to open the passenger door of his car. He noticed the van started to slowly drive away.

Gabriel kicked Nick's arm and managed to squirm out of the passenger side. Nick dove after Gabriel, but his belt buckle caught onto the stick shift.

"Come on, come on, come on!" Kit shouted at Gabriel while holding the side door open. Gabriel caught up to the moving van and tossed the bag at Kit. Kit was quick to react and caught the bag.

"I've always wanted to do this," Gabriel said just before leaping towards the moving van. Kit grabbed the back of Gabriel's coat and yanked him inside the van. Heidi caught Gabriel and pulled him away from the door.

"Hammer it!" Gabriel exclaimed as he tumbled on top of Heidi. Blake sped off full throttle while Nick followed after them on foot. Some of the other teenagers from inside ran after them too; their cheers and chants were indistinctive.

"I'll kill all of y'all!" Nick shouted, his eyes burning with rage. Once Blake got the van on the main road, they escaped Nick's chase with ease. Everyone in the get-away van began laughing hysterically.

"This was fun, let's do it again sometime," Heidi humored. She held Gabriel's head to her chest. Gabriel closed his eyes.

The five of them drove south from Portland with no agenda and no plan. Gabriel had a hard time grasping all that was happening. He was exhausted from all the adrenaline, yet excited to be this reckless for the first time in his life. It wasn't like him to be this way, yet he welcomed this recklessness like a familiar friend. The rush was worth it all, and Heidi was there to complete the feeling.

"I can hardly believe I'm in a stolen van with you guys. You're the craziest group of savages I've ever met!" Gabriel exclaimed.

"Yeah buddy!" Blake shouted with a raspy voice.

Gabriel kept his arm where he felt it belonged, around Heidi. The moment took no effort to enjoy. The sound of everyone's laughter blended with the music in Gabriel's head. He looked at Blake and his messy dark hair, then Heidi who was giggling like a gossiping schoolgirl, and he whispered under his breath, "This is where I want to be."

Everyone praised Gabriel for orchestrating such a radical escape, but Gabriel's focus was preoccupied. In this very moment, all that his mind could ponder was the electric love that coursed through his veins. Heidi's presence was like a painkiller to his soul. The crew was still shouting, but their voices became inaudible to Gabriel when he hugged Heidi once more.

"I think I love you," Heidi spoke softly as she rested her head against Gabriel's chest and closed her eyes.

Gabriel enveloped her with his embrace and kissed the top of her head.

"So now what, though?" Auston asked when everyone simmered down. Blake looked into the mirror and stared directly at Gabriel.

"You gonna tell 'em?" Blake asked. Gabriel took a moment to gather his thoughts. "Oh yeah, guys, so my dad uh—" he began explaining.

"Gabriel has a lot of money," Blake interrupted.

"Uh yeah—what he said," Gabriel chuckled.

"How much is a lot?" Kit asked.

"Ladies and gentlemen," Gabriel announced as he opened his bag, "This is what three-hundred thousand dollars in cash looks like." Everyone's eyes caught fire when they saw the thick cash stack in Gabriel's bag. They were like a congress of monkeys spotting the last remaining banana on a tree.

"I thought you said you had a hundred grand," Blake spoke up.

"I said it's over a hundred," Gabriel replied.

"Why are we still here?" Kit laughed. "Let's get out of here! We could be partying and we're just sitting here, let's go!" Gabriel hesitated to speak up, but with everyone waiting so eagerly to hear what he had to say, Gabriel gave in.

"Ah what the heck," he flaunted, "You guys wanna go to Vegas?"

"Um, yeah!" Kit shouted. Everyone else in the van cheered along. In an instant, Gabriel was no longer riding in a stolen van, but rather a party bus heading to the enchanting, Las Vegas.

"Yeah, I don't think I love you—" Heidi said to Gabriel as she held him tightly. "I definitely love you now."

Chapter 7

"Almost there, guys," Blake said to the drowsy squad of runaways. The evening sun was getting close to hiding itself behind the horizon. Auston and Kit were still in the back, passed out on each other like a romantic couple. Gabriel carefully scooted from under Heidi's cuddle, trying not to wake her, and seated himself on the passenger seat.

"You can keep sleeping if you want," Blake told Gabriel.

"I wasn't even sleeping."

"Oh, like—The whole time?" Blake asked. Gabriel nodded yes; his eyes were shutting involuntarily.

"Dude, are you serious, the whole time?" Blake complained lightly.

"Yeah, I've just had a lot on my mind," Gabriel said.

"Well—I'm stupid tired."

"Did you want me to drive?"

"Nah, I can make it now. We're only a few minutes away anyway," Blake said, "I'm just saying that it'd be nice if like, you drove earlier."

"I'm stupid, too," Gabriel slurred, "—I mean, I'm stupid tired, too."

"Well, you're pretty stupid too," Blake humored, "—let's be honest."

"Hah, screw you man," Gabriel snickered along with Blake.

"So… you and Heidi, huh?" Blake asked.

"I guess so, man—I guess so," Gabriel sighed deeply.

"I never would have thought that she would like someone like you."

"You think it's because of all the money I've got?"

"No, you're just wild and she digs that. Since the last time I saw you, you've become all crazy—like, you're down to do crazy stuff and that's… unusual." Blake explained.

"I think that's just what Portland does," Gabriel joked, "I remember the first time you left Seattle, you were such a good little kid—we all were."

"Yeah… that's what life does to you." Blake agreed.

"Pretty much—and drugs too," Gabriel nodded his head in a comedic fashion.

"Bah! It's not the drugs that changed me," Blake said.

"I know, I was just kidding—but still, when you went to Portland the first time all those years ago, you came back way different. I'm not saying it was drugs but I'm also not saying it was not drugs."

"I have a perfectly good explanation," Blake corrected, "I met Nick after you-know-what happened with my parents, and he showed me all kinds of things that I never knew were possible for someone my age. I mean, yeah—he's a terrible guy for giving me drugs, but still—I learned a whole deal about the world that Seattle never taught me."

"And you sucked me into it," Gabriel added.

"You brought yourself here, I had no idea you were even coming." Blake countered.

"True—true."

"I gotta ask, why did you leave Seattle?"

"I got this money from my dad and I just—I don't know, man. It's hard to explain. I guess when you have like a hundred different things going on in your head and then someone gives you a way out, you take it. I think that's what this is, it's my way out."

"Why would your dad give you three hundred grand?"

"Inheritance money—I was supposed to save it for when I bought a house."

"So you had three hundred grand that you never told me you had?"

"I didn't know about it, either," Gabriel responded, "I'm actually surprised he gave it to me so easily."

"What do you mean?" Blake asked.

"After I broke up with Lily, I went to the hospital to tell my dad that I needed my money, and he just… gave it up."

"Wait—I didn't know you and Lily were dating," Blake said, "—And why is your dad in the hospital?"

"Dang, you missed a lot, huh?"

"Yeah, evidently,"

"Well, my dad had a heart attack two days ago, and was hospitalized."

"Seriously? What happened?" Blake slowed the speed of the van slightly.

"I really don't know. It happened when I was fighting with Sam. I guess he just has a weak heart."

"That's so sad—I'm sorry, bro."

"It's no big deal," Gabriel responded.

"It sort of should be a big deal though, don't you think?" Blake noted.

"Well yeah, I guess it is serious and all. I just really had to leave Seattle."

"Why, though?"

"Lily said it best—things in my life are just moving too fast."

"But like, what exactly?" Blake asked.

"Bro, I just can't be there anymore. Everything stresses me out, and when I really need someone, no one is there for me," Gabriel had a slight quiver in his voice "—And the worst part is that nobody cares to try and understand me. Oh sure, everyone offers their help, but I don't need help. All I want is to be taken seriously and be heard. You know what I mean? I just wanna be heard, but instead, people just try to fix me."

Blake listened attentively to Gabriel vent, and that's what Gabriel was touched by most; being listened to.

"I feel you," Blake said.

"I mean, it's whatever now," Gabriel continued, "She was the only one who listened, but she's out of the picture now."

"Oh yea, so what happened with you two?" Blake asked, "I didn't even know you guys were together."

"Dude, it's crazy," Gabriel said with a burst of excitement, "So after you left, Lily and I hung out a few times, and it was all going great. The thing is, I got the inheritance and I was just so done with everything that I wanted to leave, but obviously I couldn't do that because of Lily."

"Aw, were you two in love?" Blake mocked.

"No dude, I'm being serious—things were going great, but we didn't know each other long enough."

"Do you still like her?"

"I mean—" Gabriel looked back to see if Heidi was awake. "I guess I sort of do. It's hard to explain," he continued. "We had a connection—I swear it was real—but then I found out that she doesn't like me and—I don't know."

"It's always been that way with you, hasn't it?" Blake added.

"Yeah, you would think I'd be used to it by now, but Lily isn't like anyone I've ever met. Everything about her makes me feel like we've known each other forever."

"That means she's a keeper," Blake said.

"I know, I know, but it was just such bad timing."

"Right person, wrong time."

"Maybe—it doesn't matter now."

"Well, if she is the right one, then she'll take you back," Blake said.

"Doubt it," Gabriel replied, "We hardly know each other, and after asking her to run away with me, I think I scared her away for good."

"You asked her to run away with you?" Blake chuckled.

"Yep."

"Dude… you really are stupid," Blake humored.

"Hah, probably."

"Wow, I'm not even surprised," Blake said. He pointed in front of his windshield and slowly said, "Would ya look at that."

"Is that Vegas?"

"Yeah buddy, that's it—that's Vegas baby."

Gabriel leaned to the edge of his seat as he glared at the wonderful glow of the city.

"It's not as magical as I thought it'd be," Gabriel commented.

"Well, it will probably look better in a few hours when it gets dark," Blake replied.

"Hey guys, wake up!" Gabriel exclaimed.

"We're here?" Heidi asked as she awoke, "Oh hey, Vegas," she said mid-yawn.

"Hey Kit! Auston!" Gabriel shouted. Neither Kit nor Auston responded. "Guys?" Gabriel spoke out again.

"Wait, be quiet," Heidi interrupted "We have to prank them. Trust me, they're heavy sleepers."

"Good idea, I'll record," Gabriel said.

"No, that wouldn't be fun."

"Well, what do you consider a funny prank?" Gabriel asked. Heidi brought herself up to Blake.

"Blake, pull-over at the next liquor store."

"Why?" Blake asked.

"Yeah, why a liquor store?" Gabriel added.

"Just—don't argue," Heidi stated.

"There's a whole bunch of liquor stores, which one you want?" Blake asked.

"Doesn't matter—there's one—pull in there." Heidi pointed towards a rundown plaza that was a block away.

"Oh my god, Heidi. This is a waste of time," Gabriel complained.

"Here's what you're going to do," Heidi said, disregarding what Gabriel comment completely, "You're going to go into that store, and you're going to bring back as much alcohol as you can handle—then I'll tell you what the rest of the plan is."

"I'm not twenty-one, though," Gabriel said.

"Then you'll have to find a way—just get it, okay?"

"You mean steal it?"

"Hh-yeah, I guess so," Heidi let out a devilish grin.

"No way, dude."

"Gabe, just do what the lady says," Blake interjected.

110

"Yeah do what the lady says—Gabe," Heidi added, putting heavy emphasis on her last word.

"Is it even worth it?" Gabriel asked.

"Of course it is!" Heidi pushed Gabriel.

"I—I can't believe I'm actually going to do this," Gabriel said, as he prepared to hop out of the passenger door.

"Oh my god, he's actually doing it!" Heidi squeaked, "I'm so excited—this is gonna be great!"

"Just hurry up, we're almost downtown!" Blake said.

"Alright, but you wait here." Gabriel climbed out of the van.

"Obviously I will. Just go already."

"I'm just saying."

"Gabe—go!" Blake exclaimed.

Gabriel dragged his feet all the way to the store entrance. He heard Heidi's cheers coming from the van, but they certainly didn't cheer him up. Upon entering the store, Gabriel was greeted by the clerk. The man was in his late twenties with a leather bound cabbie hat, and a rather kind look in his eyes. Despite his harmless appearance, Gabriel was still afraid.

"Can I help you with something?" the clerk asked.

"Um, no I'm alright," Gabriel said timidly.

"Okay, no problem, you just let me know if I can do anything for you."

"S—sounds good, sir. Thank you, sir," Gabriel mumbled. He continued through the aisle, walking as if he was being followed by a pack of wild hyenas. Anxiety mastered him when he noticed all of the varieties of alcoholic beverages. All the sizes and colors of the drinks propagandizing themselves made Gabriel panic, he already dreaded his decision to come.

"You alright, bud?" The clerk asked as he walked up to stock a refrigerator. Gabriel ducked out of sight, breathing heavily. He knew he had little time left to pick what to steal. *"What if Heidi doesn't like that kind?"* he stressed. He could hear steps coming towards him; each step was perpetually getting louder. Out of deep angst, Gabriel grabbed ahold of the largest assortment of drinks he spotted and dashed towards the exit.

"W—whoa hey!" The clerk hollered.

"I'm so sorry!" Gabriel screamed as he sprinted with all his might. The clerk chased after Gabriel, but couldn't keep up with those swift ostrich legs.

"Blake, start the van!" Gabriel shouted repeatedly "Start the van, start the van, start the van!"

Heidi kept the side door propped open. The clerk abandoned his chase only half-way across the parking lot. He hurled his cabbie hat at Gabriel just as Gabriel was jumping into the van.

"Don't come back!" The clerk yelled.

Blake sped off, plowing over the sidewalk and into the street. The bus shook side to side like a wild bull. Gabriel dropped the case of beer on the seat and tackled Heidi.

"Oh my god, I can't believe you actually stole it!" Heidi said.

"Don't ever make me do that again," Gabriel responded as he gripped his hair with both hands.

"Okay lame-o."

"Hey look who woke up!" Blake announced. Gabriel turned to the back of the van and saw Kit waving hello with one hand and rubbing his eye with the other.

"Is Auston awake?" Gabriel asked.

"Nope," Kit responded.

"I don't get how he can still be sleeping," Gabriel said. Kit, who was right beside Auston, shrugged his shoulders.

"Come on Gabey-wavey, grab a drink before Auston wakes up," Heidi urged.

"And do what?" Gabriel responded.

"For the prank—you silly-hillbilly."

"You still haven't said what the prank is."

"Obviously pour it on his head—duh!" Heidi giggled.

"Why would—how is that even funny?" Gabriel reasoned.

"Because it just will be… I know Auston and you don't."

"Exactly!" Gabriel shouted, "I don't know him!"

"Hush," Heidi said.

"Dude—why are you making me do this stuff?" Gabriel continued, nervously looking back at Auston.

"Here," Heidi handed Gabriel an open beer-bottle. Gabriel grabbed it and trembled as he held it.

"I don't want to be here for this," Kit said as he got up and moved away from Auston. Gabriel swallowed his jitters, leaped over a row, and emptied the bottle over Auston's head. Auston gagged and gasped from sudden shock and Gabriel flinched as well. He lost grip of the bottle and dropped it, hitting Auston's head with a loud clonk.

"Gah—What the hell, man?" Auston screamed, rubbing his head. Gabriel laughed madly, along with everyone else in the van.

"Dude—I'm sorry, man," Gabriel snorted.

"What is this?" Auston complained, referring to the liquid that drenched his long, frizzy hair.

"It's beer—stupid," Heidi shouted.

"Why did you pour beer on me, man?" Auston complained.

"That wasn't cool—I know—I'm sorry," Gabriel replied.

"It's all over my shirt now, and this is the only shirt I have—I left everything back at Nick's."

"I feel terrible—I'm seriously sorry," Gabriel apologized.

"Gabe, you really should get him a new shirt," Blake suggested.

"Wow—yeah okay, that's totally fair that I have to pay for something that you—" Gabriel pointed at Heidi, "—made me do."

"Me?" Heidi gasped. "What?"

"Yeah you. Whatever," Gabriel looked to Auston, "I'll get you a new shirt, bro."

"I don't want you to get me a new shirt," Auston grimaced.

"I said I'm sorry—it was just a prank."

"Whatever dude."

"Let me give you some cash and you can get yourself something nice," Gabriel offered. Auston just kept squeezing the liquid out of his hair. Gabriel retrieved the stack of cash from his bag and pulled out several hundred-dollar bills. "There—that's like a grand," He handed it. Auston stared at the money for a few moments before taking it like a dog snatching a bone.

"Hey, I want a grand," Heidi whined.

"You're the one who made me spill beer on him," Gabriel said. He looked at Kit, and Kit appeared to be on the same side with Heidi. "You know what? I'll give all y'all a grand, and then you have to promise to not bug me about money again—Agreed?" Heidi and Kit nodded their heads with massive grins on their faces. "I'm serious," Gabriel added.

"Of course, love." Heidi smiled from cheek to cheek. Gabriel counted out thousand dollar stacks and handed them out to Heidi, Kit, and then Blake.

"Here Auston—take this," Gabriel gave another thousand dollars, "—and grab yourself a beer."

Auston seemed unimpressed, but still took the offer. The teenagers then consumed the alcohol like hungry piranha. The itch to feel free from Lily eventually produced a rage in Gabriel, and the alcohol he drank added just enough confidence to act on it. All of them took wildly to the streets like madmen, crashing into everything in their path. They screamed at the top of their lungs without reason, and the rest of the night slowly faded into a blur.

When Gabriel woke up, he was dazed and uncomfortable. As his focus was restored, he realized he was lying under the van with gravel poking at his back. He crawled out, wondering how he even got there while intoxicated, when it took this much effort to get out sober. Heidi was in the van with Kit and Auston. Gabriel stepped in and pounded on the ceiling until they woke up.

"You guys know where Blake is?" He asked.

Kit groaned, while Auston and Heidi just held their heads in pain. Gabriel asked again. Just then, a noise came from the passenger seat. Gabriel looked over the front passenger seat and saw Blake laying there with his feet up and his head under the glove compartment.

"You good?" Gabriel asked. Blake moaned and waved his hand at Gabriel to leave him.

"Where in the world are we?" Heidi asked, her eyes closed. Gabriel looked around and couldn't recognize anything.

"I'm pretty sure we're still in Vegas," he replied.

"What happened?" Heidi asked with a dull voice.

Nobody could give a solid answer to that question. Judging by all the empty beer bottles, and some not empty, they figured it was safe to assume they had partied a little past their bedtime.

"Hey guys, check this out," Auston announced. "—It's oxy."

"Oh, look who actually woke up," Gabriel joked.

"Dude no way!" Kit leaned in. "Did we seriously take that?"

"Yeah and check this out," Auston replied, "—They're eighty-milligram pills." He pinched a pill and held it up in the light.

"That sure explains this then," Blake spoke up from the front.

"What? Let me see," Gabriel asked. His faced thrilled when he saw Blake's arm. "Looks like... a bunch of phone numbers."

"Whose numbers are these?" Blake freaked.

"I don't think anyone remembers a thing from last night."

"Does anyone know the time?" Heidi asked.

"Four-thirty," Gabriel responded.

"Dude I don't know what we did last night," Blake said as he took a half empty bottle of beer "but I'm down to do it again." He chuckled and chugged the remainder of the bottle.

"Oh guys—I just remembered I have some Xannies," Heidi announced.

"What's that?" Gabriel asked innocently.

"What's-what?" Heidi replied, "—You mean Xanax?" Gabriel shrank away from Heidi, covering his nervous smile. "Oh my—you don't know what Xanax is—that's adorable!" Heidi squeaked.

"Hey—I've been sheltered my entire life... but I'm down to try whatever."

"Nobody say what it does," Blake added.

"Why? What does it do?" Gabriel looked around. Blake laughed under his breath, indicating Gabriel wasn't going to get any information out of him. "Fine then—I'll only do it if you guys do it with me," Gabriel said. Auston and Kit both raised their hands. Gabriel looked at them with a peculiar smile. "Are we really doing this again?"

"Yeah buddy!" Blake forced a side hug on Gabriel. His alcoholic breath went straight up Gabriel's nostrils.

Auston and Kit started off before everyone, consuming Xanax and drinking booze. It wasn't long before Heidi joined in as well. Once Kit brought Oxycodone into the mix, things were off to a wicked start. The day progressed into another night of partying. This time around, the partying didn't stop with just a few drinks and painkillers. They scrammed in and out of the main strip downtown and the outskirts of the city, breaking through bars and picking fights. The squad was gradually morphing into more of a barbarian-like troop than just a wild group of runaways. The lust of their hearts pulled them through the most treacherous of places that Sin City had to offer, and things turned to a blur quicker than the night before.

When Gabriel woke up, it became evident to him just how extreme his new friends could party. His headache was twice the caliber as the night before, and there were muscles he didn't even know he had that were sore. The van was completely trashed; it looked like someone had turned on a massive blender full of garbage, and forgot to put a lid on it. Heidi and Auston were secretively discussing something in the back row. Gabriel didn't bother to interject, but he did wonder. He picked up his journal and looked at it for a moment.

"Hey," Blake said from the driver's seat, "So... we need to talk."

"My head... I think it's broken—it hurts so bad," Gabriel moaned.

"Last night, Kit went missing—well, actually we know where he is but, yeah," Blake continued.

"Ugh—wait, can you say all that again," Gabriel responded, battling his hangover.

"Kit got arrested last night," Blake said bluntly. Gabriel squeezed his eyes shut tighter as he tried to think about what Blake was telling him.

"Arrested?" Gabriel asked.

"Pretty much."

"For what?"

"I think—I think maybe you should just see this," Blake stuttered. He handed Gabriel a phone. Gabriel noticed Blake's forearm had even more numbers written in ink than the night before. The phone Blake held was playing a video, and Gabriel was terrified at first glance seeing his own face displayed and it was covered in blood marks.

"Is that me?" Gabriel asked.

"Hold up—you gotta see this next part," Blake said. Gabriel squinted his eyes to focus in on the video. He saw that Kit was beside him in the video, also with blood marks on his face. They seemed to be somewhere outside, somewhere like behind a strip mall.

"What are we doing?"

"—Just watch."

As the video progressed, Kit suddenly sprung from the place he stood and began fighting with what appeared to be a homeless man.

"Holy—is that Kit?" Gabriel gasped. Following after Kit, Gabriel threw a punch at the man that Kit was fighting. Next thing, two other people, one man and one woman, tried to pull Gabriel and Kit off the man being beaten. Gabriel shoved the woman away and proceeded to lunge kick the man. Kit landed a nose-breaking punch to the homeless man on the ground.

"Who are they?" Gabriel stressed. Blake remained silent until the video finished, and it finished with bright red and blue lights flashing.

"My guess is that they were just some random homeless people. I think that you two took too much Xanax," Blake replied.

"How come I don't remember any of this?"

"I'm not sure, but you did it," Blake shrugged, "—and Kit is the only one who got caught."

Gabriel gripped the hair on the back of his head.

"So yeah. Kit left a voicemail on my phone and said that he got arrested and needs to be bailed out," Blake continued "The call came from the correctional facility."

"Okay yeah—I'll bail him out," Gabriel nodded.

"You better," Blake puffed, "You were the one to start the whole thing."

"Blake, actually—Let me think for a second," Gabriel said. Blake had started the van and was ready to drive. He looked back at Gabriel. "—We can't get Kit right now."

"We have to—he's waiting for us," Blake stressed.

"I know, I know," Gabriel said, "—But just think for a moment."

"Oh my god, why?" Blake rolled his eyes. "While you are thinking about it, Kit is waiting for us," Blake continued as he put the van into gear.

"No stop!" Gabriel exclaimed, "We can't go because we don't know if the cops are looking for us, too."

"What?" Blake uttered, "Nobody is looking for us—chill."

"No, I'm serious, Blake."

"—And I'm serious, too. Kit is in jail because of you, and we're gonna get him out."

"Because of me?" Gabriel addressed, "You don't know that—and what if we show up and they arrest us on the spot?"

"You're not gonna get arrested, stupid."

"Obviously I will, since they have evidence against us."

"No, they don't."

"Then how did Kit get arrested?" Gabriel questioned.

"Because Kit is a slow runner," Blake opined.

"No way am I going to go bail him out—not right now," Gabriel said sternly. Blake smacked the steering wheel full force, yelling, "Kit is my friend!"

Gabriel flinched. Heidi and Auston's whispers were suddenly silenced.

"I mean… he's my friend, too," Gabriel said.

"No, he's not," Blake interrupted, "You don't know him like we do."

"That's not really fair."

"What's not fair is you not bailing him out when you're the one that picked on those homeless people in the first place."

"How do you know that? You don't even know." Gabriel argued.

"Dude… just bail him out."

"I'm not going to jail too, Blake," Gabriel said. Without warning, Auston put Gabriel in a firm headlock. Gabriel immediately reacted by kicking his legs back and forth, and used his hands to try to loosen Auston's grip. Heidi began shouting, and Blake was quietly watching. Gabriel started smacking Auston with his journal and twisted his hips until he was able to escape the headlock.

"What's wrong with you?" Gabriel screamed, wheezing and coughing. Auston stood up, his head was pressed against the ceiling of the van. Gabriel didn't stand up to Auston. Instead, he furiously kicked the side door open and leaped out of the van.

"Where you going, Gabe?" Blake shouted. Gabriel didn't look back. He stormed off in the heat of the moment, whispering curses under his breath. He could hear the van horn honking, and then moments later, the van drove off. Gabriel glanced back for a split second. Neither Auston nor Heidi looked back at him. Gabriel leered at them as they sped off.

Not even a minute passed when Gabriel came to the realization that he had left his bag in the van. Immediately, he reached for his phone and called Heidi. He figured Heidi was the only one with whom he didn't have a conflict with, so she'd be able to convince Blake to come back. Gabriel waited, but Heidi didn't answer; not the first time, not even the third time he called. Gabriel decided he would call Blake next. Sure enough, Blake didn't answer, either. By this point, Gabriel was panicked. In a desperate attempt, he called Auston. Auston didn't answer, and so Gabriel tried calling Heidi again.

When Heidi didn't answer the final time, reality sunk in that the very friends he ran away with had abandoned him. Now there he was, left in a city he wasn't familiar with, with nothing but the clothes he wore and his journal. Afraid, yet full of rage, and vengeful, yet paranoid; Gabriel dashed off. He ran full sprint onto the interstate and mindlessly continued running from the city. Terrified, all he wanted at this point was to be as far away from the city as possible, considering his best friend had just ditched him and he was probably wanted by the police.

Eventually, Gabriel slowed his pace. After running for what felt like hours, he dropped to his knees. Never had he felt this defeated in his life. Never was it this hard to breathe, and not only because his lips were parched and his throat was bone-dry. Never had Gabriel desired to cease existing like he did in this moment. He coughed uncontrollably as he struggled to catch his breath. A stabbing pain in his stomach gripped Gabriel. He placed his hand where the pain was.

"I'm never doing drugs again," Gabriel cringed.

The sound of crumpling gravel resounded behind Gabriel. He opened his eyes and looked ahead of him, noticing that there were headlights illuminating the setting before him. He cautiously turned his head to see who pulled over. To his relief, the vehicle wasn't a police car, but rather a white pick-up truck. Gabriel stood up when the driver's door opened. Then an elderly man wearing a blue baseball cap peeked over the door.

"You alright there, son?" The man asked.

"Yeah I'm—" Gabriel coughed, "I'm fine... s— sir."

"Where ya headed?"

"Uh... To be honest, I'm not sure how to answer that question," Gabriel replied, holding his hand up in front of his face to block the rays omitting from the headlights.

"You're runnin'—" The man called out, "I recognize when a man's runnin'."

"I'm not, though," Gabriel responded.

Yeah you are—c'mon and get in, son," the man said. His voice was calm and welcoming. He sat back into his truck then leaned across the passenger seat to prop open the door. Gabriel didn't hesitate very long.

"What makes you think I'm running?" Gabriel asked as he eased himself into the truck.

"Well, you aint the first lost soul I seen on this here highway," the man replied with a heavy southern accent. Gabriel kept himself from looking at the man as he was both ashamed and intimidated. "Now, I can take you as far as Salt Lake City. Then you're on your own," the man continued.

"Yeah, that'd be great," Gabriel said, "—I'm Gabriel, by the way."

"I don't care who you are," the man replied. "Not so long as you don't know who you yourself are."

"Well uh…" Gabriel replied, feeling as awkward as can be, "—What should I call you?"

"You call me 'Sir.'"

"Well, sir… thanks for stopping for me."

Gabriel rested his head against the window. The piercing thought of his mother's gaze made him quiver. There seemed to be a strange connection between his mother and Lily. It was almost as though Lily had possessed Gabriel's mother's spirit. Something about the way Lily spoke was enough to make him crumble instantly. He longed to understand why she made him feel this way, but he forced himself to stop thinking about her so that he could get over her sooner.

Chapter 8

"Get up," Gabriel heard a voice trespassing his dreams. "Get up, son." The voice continued to echo inside his head. Gabriel flinched violently when he felt a nudge against his shoulder wake him.

"I'm sorry, I just really needed a nap," Gabriel said to the man he'd been hitching a ride with.

"A nap's when you catch some shut-eye before supper after you've been pickin' blueb'rrys all mornin'," the man said, "But you done slept since before we reached Arizona."

"Oh dang, are we that far already?" Gabriel asked rhetorically. He noticed a horrid stench from inside the truck. The smell partnered with the blast of heat that came from the front facing vents to make the scent all the more fowl.

"What's that smell?" Gabriel plugged his nose.

"You mean that puke smell?" the man replied snidely.

"Yeah—what is it?"

127

"Well I'll tell ya what that is. That right their puke belongs to you. Yep—done let it out all over the floor there while you was snoozing."

Gabriel lifted his legs up in horror the moment he noticed, what was purportedly, his own vomit on the truck floor.

"Oh my god!" Gabriel exclaimed.

"Now, now, don't you use that name in vain," the man said. His forehead turned red, and the speed of the vehicle seemed to increase slightly.

"Sorry, it's just, so gross."

"Mhmm-You're right about that."

"Did I really throw up?"

"You're sittin' in it, aint ya?"

"How come I don't remember?"

"You don't remember what?" the man replied harshly, "—spitin' yer stomach juices all over the floors? Dad-gummit!"

"I—I'm sorry but like—I legit don't remember that happening!"

"I'll tell ya—we was still on the interstate when you just lifted your head up real fast n' puked," the man grumbled "then you dropped your head right back where it was on the arm rest n' slept all the rest of the way."

"Ew that's—I'm so sorry… sir."

"I don't know what you was doing there in Las Vegas, but you ought to steer clear of that town—least 'til yer body's mended."

"Oh, I for sure won't be going anywhere near that place again," Gabriel replied "I don't even know how something like this can happen," he said, knowing that it was because of all the alcohol and other substances he consumed.

"Well, that's Vegas for ya," the man replied, "Now look'ey there," he pointed with his nose "you see that lil' rundown diner right there?"

"Yeah," Gabriel responded.

"Thas' far as I can take ya."

The man pulled over at the diner. From the corner of his eye, Gabriel noticed the man's fingers slightly trembling. "Here we are," the man announced as he parked the truck and applied the brake.

Gabriel approached the diner with caution. The diner itself looked like it had been vacated for years. There was an old grubby payphone outside, and a few cars were parked between it and the gas station. The windows of the diner were hazed. His skepticism increased when he noticed every out-of-order sign loosely hanging across each pump.

"Listen here." the man turned to Gabriel. "Now the gentleman inside, his name is 'Butch.' He owes me money."

"Butch?" Gabriel repeated under his breath.

"Right—now, I'm going to help you out, son. I can't tell you why, but I'll do it."

"Why can't you te— "

"Listen here, boy!" the man barked, "There's a bit too much to explain, so I'll take the liberty of explaining only what you ought to know."

Gabriel froze in in his tracks. He was spooked. Each of his arm hairs stood up, and his tongue glued itself to the top of his mouth. The man's unexpected wrathful tone stunned Gabriel into submission. He stared at the man's eyes as they gradually turned bloodshot-red.

"Now I'm going in there and talking to the man that owns this establishment, while you, son, are gon' wait out here."

The man promptly entered the diner, while Gabriel remained in the exact same posture. After a minute of waiting in the cold, Gabriel saw the man storm out of the diner.

"Alrighty boy! Now, Butch agreed to provide you with employment. Albeit, he's not the cleanest pig in pen, but he's got a nice little place in the back where you can stay during the night n' a job to do during the daytime. I know I aren't able ta—take ya any farther, so if you're not gon' stay here, then you ought to seek refuge elsewhere."

Gabriel, blank-faced, replied, "I don't even know what to say." The man sighed deeply as he leaned in.

"Look, boy," He spoke softly, "There's something you don't know about any of this, about me, but I'll tell you what—right now you just do what you believe to be right." He placed his hand on Gabriel's shoulder. "If ya think on it, thas-all that makes a man really—when you decide it's time to become one." He smiled and began walking away

"Oh, and little Gabe!" The man turned around. "—The name's Amos."

"Wait, hold on!" Gabriel shouted as Amos climbed back into his truck. Amos, despite being the old and leisurely man he was, was quick to flee the scene. "I... I have questions," Gabriel called out, as he watched Amos drive off on his white pick-up.

"You the kid?" A gravelly voice asked from behind. Gabriel immediately knew whose voice it was. Butch stood seven feet tall. His gray tank top stretched over his belly, covering most of it. He was sucking on a lollipop, as a droplet of drool tipped off the end of the lollipop stick and stained his tank.

"Yeah, that's me," Gabriel said, stretching his hand out.

"Get in—lot of dirty dishes to do," Butch turned his back. His massive physique swayed him side to side with each step he took. Gabriel slowly lowered his hand, repulsed by the self-satisfied smirk on Butch's face.

The smell of burnt grease and harsh cleaning chemicals were the first things Gabriel noticed when he entered the diner. A chime rang as he stepped foot inside, and it drew the attention of some of the guests. Judging by the grandfather clocks, ragged booths, artificial flowers, and partially-torn wallpaper, Gabriel presumed this diner was once a delightful and welcoming place before Butch degraded it.

"Ah'right, so you're gonna work the dishes tonight, and I'll be showing you how to work the register tomorrow," Butch began explaining, slurring his words and belching between sentences "Um… c'mere. I'll show you the back where you're gonna stay."

"It's so quiet. Where are the rest of the workers?" Gabriel asked.

"Let's get one thing straight, all right?" Butch retorted, "I'll be doing all the talking. You are lucky enough that I fired the other guy last month and so you'll be taking his position as long as you don't talk as much as that bastard did."

"Well I don't even know if— "

"What did I just say?" Butch asked with a condescending tone.

"I'm just saying, I don't even know if I want— "

"You got any bags?" Butch interrupted again.

"Not really," Gabriel answered, "Just my journal."

"Then go ahead and get started on the dishes, and when they're all clean you can sleep in this room," Butch said. Gabriel walked into the room that Butch was pointing at and flipped on the light switch. The room had white brick walls and a solid concrete floor. There were metal shelves along the perimeter, and a set of laundry and dryer machines against the back wall.

"There's no bed," Gabriel stated.

"You're right—there is no bed. You can sleep on those towels though," Butch responded, pointing at a bin of soiled rags. Gabriel swallowed his saliva and timidly asked, "How about food?"

"Food?" Butch snickered, "We're in a diner, you can buy yourself whatever you want."

"When would I get paid? Because, I don't really have any money."

Butch walked to the kitchen sink and picked up a sponge. As he handed Gabriel the sponge, he said,

"If you do good... Then Friday."

Gabriel took the sponge and inched over to the sink with his head low. He was still dehydrated from throwing up earlier and was anxious to get a sip of water from the sink. "I'll be here at five t'morrow," Butch said. Gabriel nodded his head while keeping his eyes down. When he turned on the rusty faucet, it began screeching and thumping. The faucet continued to grumble for a few moments before a dense brown liquid leaked out the base of the sink. The leak ceased once water streamed out the spout. The water was brown at first, but soon turned to orange, and then clear.

"I don't think this is very sanitary," Gabriel commented sarcastically.

"What? It's clean now, just wipe it up and get the dishes started," Butch spat.

Gabriel began wiping the first dish, nauseated by the smell that emanated off it. Every inch of the plates, mugs, and silverware was covered in a buttery-grease that no amount of dish soap could break down. Dish after dish, his frustration only increased. He eventually had to resort to intense scrubbing just to get past the top layer of grime.

The rest of the day was spent there, in the confines of those four kitchen walls.

A neatly organized tower of clean dishes stood tall to Gabriel's right. Despite his excruciating thirst and drowsiness, he managed to finish tidying up. He didn't even bother turning the water off as he left the kitchen and dragged his feet all the way into the pantry room before dropping himself into the bin of rags.

Gabriel shut his eyes. His body was still recovering from the drugs. The water from the rusty sink seemed too gross to drink from, and the restroom faucet wasn't any better. He tried his best to ignore his thumping headache. He figured the sooner he could fall asleep the quicker morning would come when he could ask Butch for clean water.

Gabriel had only just shut his eyes, when Butch barged in.

"Get up kid!" Butch exclaimed as he yanked Gabriel by his ankles.

"What the heck!" Gabriel shouted.

"What the heck is exactly right," Butch retorted, "Look at this—the water is runnin' and all the tables are still dirty. You think you can sleep when you haven't finished your job yet?"

"You didn't say anything about cleaning tables!" Gabriel protested.

"I don't have time for this," Butch's massive hand gripped Gabriel's entire right shoulder and lifted him up.

"We open in five minutes!" He yelled as he launched Gabriel out of the pantry and into the cafeteria. Gabriel barely evaded crashing into the register before he could catch his balance. "You'll need this," Butch chucked a wet rag at Gabriel's chest.

"What's your problem, dude?" Gabriel mumbled, his eyebrows stiffened.

"Five minutes!"

"There's no way it's already five in the morning," Gabriel grumbled as he sloppily wiped the crumbs off the tables that yesterday's customers left behind. Butch opened the diner just after five o'clock even though there was nobody waiting at the front door. Gabriel was exasperated by Butch's urgency to have the diner cleaned, when, in fact, no one would be there to see it. Butch didn't seem to be bothered by the lack of customers, though. He was still insistent that Gabriel hurried.

As Gabriel intensely wiped the dried sauces and greasy handprints off of the tables, his right shoulder experienced a shooting soreness. He lifted his sleeve to inspect the pain and saw a peevish bruise had formed on his right shoulder where Butch had gripped him. Gabriel was more concerned with Butch however, than he was his pain. He stared at the swelling bruise for a moment, and then resumed wiping.

"Early risers are here—get in the kitchen," Butch announced. Gabriel finished the last table and hurried to get out of sight. "—And take their order after I seat them."

When the first customer entered the diner, Butch welcomed them like a friend. Gabriel patiently waited behind the kitchen wall. His eyes were dry and his stomach felt upside down. He figured the first thing he should do is bring up water, which would be a perfect opportunity to get himself some filtered water, as well. He didn't wait long before Butch entered the kitchen.

"Where's the water?" Gabriel asked.

"The sink is right there," Butch looked at Gabriel like he was stupid.

"I mean the clean water—for the customers."

Butch grabbed a cup and walked up to the faucet. He filled the cup with water and took a gulp from it. The water tunneled down his throat like a sewer drain on a rainy day.

"It's clean—here, take this to the table," Butch said as he handed Gabriel the cup he had just drank from.

"So… gross," Gabriel murmured under his breath.

Later that day, Gabriel gave in to his severe thirst and drank from the sink. He never thought so highly of his life that he left behind until now. An aching regret overcame him. As the day progressed, he recalled the moment when he silently professed his love for Lily. The smile that she had when her finger met his through the bus window replayed in his head over and over. Once again, Lily began to invade his thoughts. Gabriel repeatedly experienced episodes of extreme longing for Lily. In those random and brief instances, he was able to forget about his physical hunger. However, lacking a warm meal was much easier to bear than the sting from missing Lily. And so, Gabriel suppressed his emotions.

By the second night of being at the diner, Gabriel was severely sleep deprived. As he lay in his bed of rags, his focus was broken between the crushing sensation in his stomach and the bitter memory of Lily's voice. He was either reminiscent of her comforting gaze, or disturbed by the pain of his malnutrition. The weight of unrequited love had crushed him. He began to feel physical pain. It was like someone was choking him from inside, and the stirring in his gut added to the over-all misery he found himself in.

After three days had passed, it was finally Friday. The diner was far busier than Gabriel was used to. He spent the better portion of that morning cleaning and taking care of customers. All along, he fantasized about how he would leave as soon as he got his pay from Butch. Gabriel's plan was set: walk to the nearest town, buy himself the largest portion of blueberry crepes he could find, and then catch up on some long overdue sleep at a motel.

To this point, every customer Gabriel had served was noisy and disrespectful, but there was a particular customer he was especially repulsed by. That customer sat in the corner booth every morning and ordered the same meal each time: chicken wings and a side of mayonnaise. Whenever Gabriel would bring up the order, the customer never failed to complain. It was always either not enough sauce on the wings, or something else arbitrary. Gabriel nicknamed the customer, "Swine," because of how much resemblance there was between the customer and an actual swine.

Noon rolled around quickly, and the breakfast rush was now over. All of the tables looked sparkling clean, and every customer had gone; all except Swine. Gabriel dreaded approaching Swine, but reminded himself that this would be the last time he'd have to deal with all the complaining. He took the bundles of used napkins and the plate of half-eaten chicken wings off of Swine's table and hurried back to the kitchen. Swine hurled a few complaints as per usual, but Gabriel shut out all of the noise and pictured himself eating blueberry crepes instead.

Once Gabriel was in the kitchen, he set the plate on the counter and began cleaning the dishes in the sink as fast as he could. He wanted the diner to be as tidy as it could be before asking Butch for the week's compensation.

When Gabriel was down to the final plate, Swine's plate, he hesitated to clean it. Noticing all the meat that was still on the bones, Gabriel thought it looked too filling to be disposed of. He glanced into the cafeteria and saw Swine leaving.

"Goodbye forever," Gabriel muttered. He then lifted a piece of chicken to his nose. As revolting as it was, he wanted it. He gagged and his stomach gurgled as he held the poultry by his mouth.

"What do you think you're doing?" Butch groused.

"I was just… hungry," Gabriel dropped the chicken wing.

"Then you can buy that," Butch pointed his finger at the plate.

"B—but, you want me to pay for food that I'm supposed to throw away?"

"It don't belong to you, does it?"

"Wait, are you being serious right now?"

"Of course," Butch replied "I'm always serious about money."

"But you know I don't have any money," Gabriel said. Butch snatched the plate from Gabriel's hand and tossed the chicken into the trash along with the plate.

"Then you can't have any of my food," Butch said, "It's that simple."

"Then pay me!" Gabriel shouted, "I mean, it's Friday anyway."

"Oh, is it now?" Butch's mouth twisted into a grimace.

"Yeah... it is... it's Friday," Gabriel nodded, "You said you'd pay me on Friday."

"I didn't say I'd pay you this Friday."

"Next... week?" Gabriel asked angrily. Butch smirked as he walked right past Gabriel and bumped shoulders with him.

Infuriated, Gabriel marched into the pantry and slammed the door shut. He kicked the bin of rags with all of his might as he growled like a hound. Every nerve ending in his body felt like it had caught fire. Gabriel dropped to his knees and kissed the ground with his forehead. Moments later, he began sobbing spasmodically.

"Why am I even here?" Gabriel cried. He made a fist and hammered it against the concrete beside his head. "How did I go from having it all… to this?"

Gabriel remembered the vendors of the street paper that Leon ran. He remembered how the poorest of vendors had decent living conditions and a warm meal every night. Even on the worst of days, the vendors always had each other's company. Yet here he was, lying on the floor of, what was perhaps, the most emotionally damaging place he had ever been in.

As Gabriel recalled the luxury of the life he once had, a thought crossed his mind. He envisioned himself walking out onto the main road and letting himself be hit by a speeding vehicle. Death would be imminent and rather painless, he reasoned. Gabriel immediately pulled his phone out and dialed Noah's number.

"Pick up, pick up, pick up," Gabriel nervously repeated. "You gotta pick up, you gotta pick up."

"Hello?" Noah answered.

"Noah?" Gabriel gasped.

"Gabe—is that you?"

"Yes—Noah!" Gabriel shuddered.

"Dude w—where are you? Are you okay?" Noah stammered. The noise coming from Noah's end of the line suggested he was around a rowdy group of people.

"I'm somewhere in Utah," Gabriel replied, crying and laughing at the same time.

"What are you doing in Utah? Everyone is worried sick."

"I know man… I just, I don't know anymore." Gabriel replied, sobbing convulsively.

"Bro, are you okay?"

"I mean… No, not really," Gabriel's said, "Actually, not at all man."

"What's going on?" Noah asked, "Are you crying?"

"I lost it all!" Gabriel shouted.

"Lost what? What are you talking about?"

"The money, I lost everything!" Gabriel screamed passionately. He squeezed the phone and clenched his teeth with a pit bull-like grip. He could hear Noah on the other end of the line making noises like he was moving somewhere. Suddenly the background noises dissipated, and Noah's voice became more clear.

"Hey, tell me exactly what's going on," Noah urged.

"I messed up," Gabriel shrieked. "I can't do this anymore."

"Okay, slow down and tell me where you are right now."

"I'm in some diner in Utah somewhere," Gabriel replied.

"Some diner?" Noah sounded vexed. "—What are you doing there?"

Gabriel took a moment to collect his thoughts together, and then, more calmly began explaining,

"I hitched a ride from Vegas, and got a job at this diner, but I just—I can't be here anymore." Noah didn't say a word, but Gabriel could hear Noah breathing through the phone speaker, and that brought him comfort. "Okay, okay... I went to Portland after I left home, and I met up with Blake. He introduced me to some of his friends, and we ran away from the place they were staying, and went to Vegas, but—" Gabriel cut his words off mid-sentence.

"But what?"

"—But they stole my money. All of it," Gabriel said. "Blake took it, and now I'm in Utah, working at some diner, and my boss won't pay me, and I'm just hungry and I feel sick and—"

"Then get out of there. Why are you still there?"

"Because..." Gabriel said. He found it difficult to answer Noah's question directly. He buried his face in the palm of his hand, sighed, and admitted, "—Because it's what I deserve."

"What do you mean?" Noah asked.

"I deserve all that has happened to me. I was never a good friend to you, and I wasn't a good son to dad. I'm just a nobody and... I can't live like this anymore," Gabriel continued. "I can honestly say that I regret leaving Lily for this. I mean, if you only saw me... I'm literally like, dying out here." He held back his tears as best he could. Noah was listening attentively through it all.

"Then come home."

"I can't—I can't just go back home."

"Why not?"

"Because... I just can't."

"Tell me why."

"I'm a failure, I'm—" Gabriel shook his head side to side, "—I'm a complete failure."

"But there's no point in staying there, though," Noah reasoned.

"But after all I've done?"

"I don't know man, but the way I see it, you staying there is the failure." Noah said, "Come home—I can pay for a train ticket," Noah suggested.

"You would do that?" Gabriel's lip quivered.

"Of course bro—you're my bro." Gabriel could almost feel the warmth from Noah's face radiate off his cheek.

"I... what would I say to my dad, or Lily? Where would I stay?"

"Anywhere here is better than anywhere there," Noah replied.

"But—"

"Just don't think, okay? Just stop thinking," Noah urged. Gabriel struggled to say yes, or say anything at all. He knew, though, that Noah was completely right.

"Okay, I'll come."

"Dude, please come back. Seriously—everybody misses you."

"I gotta go," Gabriel said, "I'll call you tomorrow."

"For sure, bro—call me."

Gabriel set the phone down and took a moment to contemplate the conversation. His fingers were trembling slightly. He was nervous about Lily, and dreaded seeing Leon. Gabriel knew he was meant to do this, though. He leaped up onto his feet and went straight into the kitchen. On his way, he grabbed a to-go box and began stuffing as much fresh produce as he could fit in it. Just before walking out of the diner, Gabriel noticed the cash register. He was overcome with a desire to steal whatever was inside, but the thought was short-lived.

Gabriel sighed deeply, then proceeded to leave the diner and walk out onto the main road. He continued down the road without looking back once. By the evening, there were city lights visible ahead. Gabriel's legs were tired, and the food in his to-go box was nearly depleted, but he kept pressing on until he reached the train station. There, behind the restroom, where the sidewalk was dark and inconspicuous, Gabriel laid down and passed out, using his journal as a pillow. The decision to return to Seattle was by far more nerve-wracking than to leave it, but Gabriel had made his mind up. And so, darkness shrouded the night, and Gabriel had never felt more anxious.

Chapter 9

The Sun shyly revealed its first rays behind the mountain skyline. Gabriel awoke suddenly when a passing wind had carried a plastic bag right into his face. He quickly rose to his feet and dusted himself off before making his way to the train station ticket booth. When he got to the booth, there was nobody inside it. Gabriel studied the signage and noticed that the booth wouldn't be open until six-thirty, which was a half hour away. He found this to be a perfect time to call Noah. When Noah picked up the phone, Gabriel skipped a polite greeting and said,

"Hey I'm already—" Gabriel stopped mid-sentence as he heard Noah groan, "—Oh, did I wake you? You sound tired." He asked Noah.

"Yeah, I usually sleep until six." Noah replied with a groggy voice.

"It's already six." Gabriel retorted.

"It's five."

"Wait… it must be the time zones." Gabriel responded, "—My bad."

"It's all good—Um… so yeah, I deposited some cash in your account last night," Noah said, "—All you gotta do is buy yourself a ticket and I'll pick you up and drive you to Aunt Betty's house where your dad is."

"Okay… I can't thank you enough." Gabriel said, smiling contently.

"No need to thank me, I'm sure I'll figure out a way for you to repay me," Noah humored, "Trust me."

"Hh-yeah that's funny, but really though. I'm so thankful to have you bro and to be honest, I'm insanely scared of coming back—because of my dad and everything. I'm like—I'm even shaking right now just from talking about it."

"I'm scared with you. Everything is gonna turn out fine."

"I know, it's just that I'll have a hard time figuring things out now." Gabriel said, "Like, finding a place to stay and food and all that kind of stuff."

"That's why we have these new things called jobs."

"Well yeah, that's the plan. I'll try to convince my dad to let me work for the paper."

"Don't you think that's kind of a stretch?" Noah asked, "It's not like he's gonna be chill with you coming back."

"I know, but I don't know what else to do. I just need something immediately, and every paper I sell I get to keep the money right away so it's basically same day pay— Which, you know, I need to eat and stuff and I can't wait two weeks for a paycheck."

"I mean, okay," Noah responded.

"I have to convince him—I have no choice."

"Just knowing your dad and how strict he is—I don't think it's a good idea."

"We will just have to see, I guess."

"Take care Gabe."

"You too Noah—See you soon."

Gabriel finished his call with plenty of time to spare before the ticket booth was open. He began scavenging for coins under an espresso stand window to buy himself a meal. When he gathered a handful of coins, he noticed a homeless man leaning against the train station ticket booth. Gabriel looked into the palm of his hand and estimated he hardly had enough to purchase himself a hamburger. Even if he had enough, the meal wouldn't be big enough to satisfy his hunger. Gabriel approached the sleeping man and dumped the collected coins into the tin can that was in front of the man instead.

When the time came for the ticket booth to open, Gabriel was first in line. Fortunately, the train that would take him to Seattle was already in station and ready to depart. It was scheduled to arrive in Seattle in a day and a half. Although that was a much lengthier trip than he wished for, he didn't complain twice. At the moment, there were far more consuming thoughts occupying his mind, like coping with the fact that he would never be a better friend than Noah, and trying to come up with just the right thing to say to Leon.

Gabriel embarked. This day was the fourth day he had gone without eating anything. He reminded himself that he already made it so far and he could surely pull through another day. The train service members had offered food menus three times that day, and each time Gabriel tried to convince them he wasn't hungry. The most difficult part was being as polite in declining as he could, when on the inside he was dying.

When the Sun was already setting, Gabriel was curled up in his seat. He stared out the window and admired the beauty of every tree he passed. He thought about how every tree had its own story. How every tree started as a seed, so petite and fragile, yet there it stood erect sturdily. Inspired by how boldly the trees stretched their branches, he wondered how many storms had the trees dealt with, or how many dry seasons they lived through. Gabriel received an epiphany; it was like a thought he didn't come up with, or rather a thought that was downloaded into his mind. In this moment he knew exactly what to draw in his journal.

The dot that was in the center of the page in his journal became a seed buried deep. Starting from the dot, Gabriel traced around it, making the dot into a bold circle. Then a stem protruded from the circle which soon reached above ground. A leaf sprouted and then another leaf. As the picture became larger by scale, the stem released small branches. These branches became numerous and soon transformed the puny plant into a fully grown tree; a tree that could not be taken down easily.

Gabriel continued to look out the window while the train passed by a forest. The forest was vast; it's end was not in sight. It came to his attention that this tree was capable of producing fruit. And so, as the work of art goes, the tree brought forth its fruit. The fruit, of course, was filled with more seeds. When the wind carried these seeds throughout the fields, more stems began to sprout where the seeds landed. Those sprouts became trees that produced their own fruit. Before long, a forest emerged. It was a forest that was vast, and its end was not in sight. Each tree was unique, and each tree begot its own story. As for the first tree, it was now aged and its life was well lived.

The tree that emerged from the first seed was modeled after the tree that stood behind Aunt Betty's house; the one he and his mother used to spend time around. The tree had a handcrafted bench under it, and it over-looked a pond. The pond was populated by lily pedals, and the Sun would always set just over the pond where the trees met the sky. He spent the remainder of the evening drawing five different images representing the epiphany, and when he finished he fell asleep.

In the morning, Gabriel paced the train nervously. The train was going to arrive in Seattle soon, and he still hadn't come up with a good enough speech to present to Leon. He thought of everything from apologies, to begging. He was even willing to offer to work for free for a month as long as he would be fed.

When the brakes were applied, and the train began to stop, Gabriel looked out the window and searched for Noah. Sure enough, Noah was there leaning against his car with headphones on. Gabriel smiled when he saw Noah. As soon as the train doors opened, Gabriel rushed out to Noah.

"Thank you, thank you, thank you!" Gabriel yelled as he hugged Noah.

Noah didn't say anything, he only hugged Gabriel back. They drove off, and Gabriel took one last look at the train. Although time passed seemingly slower, he still missed being onboard. He accepted that the train ride was, in its own way, the transition from the ungrateful portion of his life, to the new. Gabriel realized the blessings he had so ignorantly left behind, and the work he would now have to put in to rebuild his life.

"How was it?" Noah broke the silence.

"The train? It was pretty good man," Gabriel replied.

"How do you feel now?"

"I'm a little freaked out, to be honest, but happy at the same time. You know?"

"Not really but—whatever you say bro," Noah replied with a rich smile on his face. Gabriel chuckled along. He didn't mention to Noah about his severe hunger. He figured if he said anything about being hungry, Noah would get him food. As nice as a meal would be, Gabriel didn't want one as he took a strange liking to being hungry. There was something about saying no to his fleshly hunger that brought out a humility in him he didn't know he had.

Gabriel took pleasure in the moment he was a part of. He was proud of himself for coming this far in his journey, and delighted in Noah being beside him even after the fight they had the last time they spoke. His future was unpredictable, and likely not an easy one to bear, but

Gabriel was content, at least in the moment. It was the first time he had felt this way in his entire life, and that alone was also something to be proud of. It was surely a pleasant atmosphere to reside in. The feeling all but withered the moment they pulled up to Leon's driveway.

"Time to go," Noah said calmly.

"Thanks again," Gabriel said as he shook Noah's hand.

"Of course," Noah replied, "I hope everything goes well with your dad."

"I—I don't even know how to feel about this." Gabriel said.

"Yeah man, you just gotta face it." Noah said. Gabriel nodded his head in agreement. "—Anyway, I have work," Noah said.

"Sounds good," Gabriel got out of the car, "See ya."

Noah drove off. Gabriel waved goodbye to him and kept waving until Noah was completely out of sight. Gabriel was hesitant of turning around and seeing the driveway he knew he was about to walk up. He looked at the gravel below his feet as he took his first few steps towards the house. It was around noon and the Sun was directly above. There were fields of tall golden grass on his left and on his right, and the sky was as clear as spring water.

Gabriel made his way up the inclined gravel and dirt road, the trees bustled in the wind. It was almost as if they were whispering to each other, and Gabriel could hear them, only he could not understand them. He imagined that if he could, that the whispers were about him and the way he would handle this moment. The way he could maintain himself before his father would determine the kind of roots he had. How if he can still hold his head high despite the utter shame he felt, that it would reveal the kind of man he was.

With each step Gabriel took, he slowed his pace. He knew that it wouldn't be easy to face Leon, but the thought that he wasn't even in sight of the house, yet was already this nervous, only furthered his anxiety. He continued to rehearse his apology, searching for ways to improve it for maximum effectiveness. His feet stumbled as often as his words stuttered. Gabriel felt that this would be his only chance at making some kind of money, and it would only happen if his speech was eloquent and heart felt. All he needed was to earn enough atonement to get the position of vendor.

"Dad, I know I failed you, and I'm sorry. There is nothing I can say or do to change that." Gabriel continually repeated his apology under his breath.

When Gabriel walked past the bend in the road, the house became visible at the very top of the hill. It was just as he remembered, a one story tall, white trim house with a porch stretching from end to end. Gabriel was still a considerable distance away, but as he stared at the house intensely, he noticed Leon sitting on the porch looking back at him. Leon sat on a white bench that he had built with Gabriel and Sam when they were still children. Leon sat up. When he looked over at Gabriel, Gabriel shivered. He slouched his shoulders and held his head low as he continued towards Leon.

"This is it, as long as I don't forget what to say and to say it loud and clear, it just might work. Oh—and don't forget to make eye contact." Gabriel thought to himself. He took deep breaths as he prepared to present himself with an apology and job request. While he was still murmuring his lines, Gabriel heard Leon's footsteps crunch on the gravel. Gabriel looked up and was caught completely off guard when he saw Leon running towards him. Gabriel stopped walking. Seeing that Leon wasn't slowing down, Gabriel braced himself. Leon reached Gabriel in a matter of seconds, casting his arms around and embracing Gabriel firmly.

"Dad I—I know I messed up," Gabriel began saying. "—And I'm so sorry for everything I've done. I'm here because I need to ask if I can please have some work... as a vendor." Gabriel continued, stammering his words and baffled as to why Leon was hugging him, "—I know I don't deserve it because of what I've done and all," His mind was racing like an engine on full throttle, "—But if you would just... hear me out... I— "

"I waited on that porch for you, every day," Leon cut Gabriel off mid-sentence.

"W-what?" Gabriel's lip quivered and his eyes moistened.

"I love you, son," Leon said, his voice was almost too subtle.

"Dad—" Gabriel said as a tear rolled down his cheek.

"Every day," Leon repeated, "I waited every day." Gabriel wanted to ask Leon why, but couldn't enunciate a single word. "I love you, son," Leon said once more.

Gabriel felt vibrations throughout his skin. It was as if the words, "I love you, son," took shape and squeezed his bones. They reverbed through the empty walls of Gabriel's heart, and became a substance that began to fill the void. Gabriel dropped his chin on Leon's shoulder and wept bitterly.

"You're home."

"Dad—" Gabriel sobbed.

"I know you left, but now you're home again," Leon spoke with a crack in his voice like he was about to cry. Gabriel wept harder, and Leon held him tighter.

"I'm so sorry!" Gabriel cried out, his voice was ugly from crying.

"I know, son," Leon responded.

"I'm so sorry for everything I've ever done!" Gabriel shouted passionately, "—And I'm not good enough to be your son."

"But you are," Leon reassured, "You are my child, and I love you."

At that, Gabriel wept his heaviest. He couldn't rid himself of the thought that he wronged Leon, but Leon's embrace made Gabriel feel like there was nothing he could do to escape this moment; this love. As he resided in the envelopment of his father, he felt his soul tear in half; and the very foundation of who he is was uprooted. Gabriel was physically too weak to say a word, and too warm inside to let go. He broke, and he kept breaking with every repeat of Leon's words in his head.

Chapter 10

"I see you still don't know how to make regular coffee," Gabriel said to Leon in a sarcastic tone as he poured himself a cup. It was mid-day, and the Sun was only going to become less bright from this point.

"You know I love my coffee strong," Leon responded, his eyes squinted and his smile kindhearted.

"Yeah but, your coffee isn't strong, it's just bitter."

"You know, you and the coffee share a lot in common,"

"What are you trying to say, that I'm bitter inside?" Gabriel chuckled.

"Strong," Leon corrected, "You're strong for coming back home and strong for accepting my forgiveness." He smiled sincerely from cheek to cheek.

"Oh, in that case—that's some dang strong coffee you got there!" Gabriel responded humorously.

"I'm very proud of you, son. I want you to know that," Leon said after a feeble laugh. His soft spoken words brought warmth to Gabriel's heart.

"So uh… Where's Sam?"

"Sam's gone. He's on a trip," Leon looked up at Gabriel, "A business trip."

"A business trip? Cool, what's it for?" Gabriel asked. Leon shrugged his shoulders, suggesting he was just as clueless as Gabriel. "You—you don't know?" Gabriel asked.

"I don't know what goes on with the company anymore," Leon said.

"What are you talking about?" Gabriel stiffened his brows.

"You haven't heard? I passed the street-paper on to Sam, I'm no longer the CEO," Leon said.

"Are you serious?"

"Yes, it's been the plan for a while now and with you leaving, and me in the hospital, I found it a good time to transition into my retirement."

"Well that's… great. I mean, really. Good for him, he worked so hard for it." Gabriel said.

"It's a shame he's going to miss out," Leon sighed.

"Miss out on what?" Gabriel asked.

"On seeing you," Leon replied.

"Sam? Missing out? I don't think so," Gabriel said.

"Of course he is going to miss out. Despite all the bickering between you two, I know he still loves and misses you—just like everyone else," Leon said. Gabriel's smile dwindled. He placed his elbows on the counter as he looked down at his hands that were clasped together.

"You think people will want to see me—still?" Gabriel asked.

"With all that you've gone through, yes of course," Leon said.

"But dad, like… After all I did?"

"You still don't get it do you, son?" Leon said. Gabriel looked deeply into Leon's eyes, gripping onto every word that came from Leon's mouth. "Ah—You'll understand when you become a father," Leon jeered, "Oh, I almost forgot—can you pick up some steak from the store? The nicest one you can find."

Just then, Gabriel's phone rang. He took it out of his pocket and placed it flat on the counter. The phone call was from Sam. Gabriel accepted the call and put it on speaker phone so that Leon can hear the conversation too.

"Hey Sam," Gabriel said cheerfully.

"So, is it true?" Sam asked Gabriel, "—Are you back?"

"Uh—yeah. I guess you can say that," Gabriel replied, "How did you know?"

"Aunt Betty called me. She said Dad's throwing you a party," Sam said. Gabriel looked at Leon with one brow raised. "What was he thinking?" Sam continued.

"I—I know. I'm just as surprised to find out as you," Gabriel said, still locking eyes with Leon.

"And you—you're just going to party it up with everyone right after coming back from, where ever it is, that you were partying?" Sam complained.

"Well, it's not like that," Gabriel said.

"How are you going to say that, when your actions prove the opposite?" Sam replied.

"Well I— "

"Sam," Leon interjected, "You should be happy."

"Happy?" Sam raised his voice, "Are you being serious right now?"

"Of course I'm being serious,"

"Dad, I have literally slaved for you all my life, and you've never celebrated me. Whatever that even means," Sam said in a mocking tone, "But when this freak son shows up after completely wasting three-hundred thousand of your dollars, you do what? You throw him a party?"

"Son, listen," Leon said.

"No dad, you listen!" Sam shouted over Leon, "That little spoiled kid does whatever he wants and always gets away with it. When are you going to do something about him?"

"I have done something about him, I let him go. But now he's back and that's why you should be as happy as I am," Leon replied.

"What has he done for you? What has he ever done for you?" Sam exclaimed, "He is nothing like me!"

"Sam, I have always loved you. Everything I have is yours, but your brother came home and all I want is for you to come home so we can all be together—Please son."

"No, that's not fair, and that's not love," Sam said belligerently just before hanging up.

"Then it seems that I have a son who is still lost," Leon said after the phone call had already ended.

"I'm sorry," Gabriel whispered as he put the phone away.

"Let me deal with it—I'm not finished with him yet. You just worry about getting that steak," Leon said as he put his hand on Gabriel's shoulder. Gabriel wanted to say something, but he knew that Leon would have wanted him to leave instead. He promptly got into Leon's car and left.

On his way back home from the grocery store, Gabriel noticed the cafe where he met Lily and something inside him called him to revisit the place. He came to the café and as he neared it, he recalled the moment they met with perfect clarity. He remembered how the rain led both of them to run frantically towards the cafe, ultimately causing them to collide like waves at the door. Although that day was gloomy and wet, it was still one the happiest of days for Gabriel.

The cafe was closed, so Gabriel didn't stick around very long. When he arrived back home, he saw that there were a few cars parked in the drive way. He was exhilarated to see that even one person showed up to see him, let alone several. Upon walking in through the front door, he was immediately welcomed by the handful of people inside. Among those people were Aunt Betty, relatives whom he hasn't seen in years, and even Brian his teacher along with numerous classmates.

"So how do you feel?" Leon asked Gabriel, pulling him in to the crowd.

"I honestly didn't expect anyone to come," Gabriel replied.

"But now that they are here, how does it make you feel?"

"Amazing," Gabriel chuckled. "Just, really amazing. Thanks for coming, everyone."

"Well there's something I want to show you," Leon said, "—Or rather, someone." Leon stretched his arm out and from around the corner came Mel. Mel walked right into Leon's arms and stole a kiss from him. Both Leon and Mel were smiling at each other like they had won the lottery. Mel then shook Gabriel's hand and introduced herself,

"Hi Gabriel. It's such a pleasure to see you again. Do you remember me?"

"Yeah, I thought you were my dad's nurse but... I guess you're much more than that now," Gabriel replied.

"Oh well, I thought so too," Mel laughed along, her hand flat on Leon's chest. She looked at Leon, "Tell him what you told me."

"Well," Leon cleared his throat, "I knew I wanted to take you out for coffee the moment you drew my blood. She kept telling me that she doesn't date patients, so I waited until I was out of the hospital to come back to her with a bouquet of roses." Leon said. He turned from Gabriel and glared into Mel's eyes, "She told me her favorite flowers were Aster's, and that it would take more than a kind gesture to woo her, but that she would still let me take her out—only because she really loved my kids."

"That's not only why I went out with you," Mel said, holding on to Leon's arm, "You made me feel comfortable."

"Well... I'm gonna let you two love birds do your thing, but um—it's a pleasure to meet you again, Mel." Gabriel nodded.

"Of course, sunshine," Mel said, her gaze beautiful and sincere.

Gabriel trailed towards the kitchen, sniffing blueberry crepes. From the corner of his eye he noticed Brian standing under the door arc to his left leaning against his walking stick. Brian's beard appeared longer than before and his infamous one-brow-raised look was exactly as Gabriel remembered. Gabriel waved to Brian and Brian acknowledged Him with a head nod. After a few moments of what seemed to be Brian trying to avoid any further eye-contact, he cracked a brief smile. Gabriel smiled back and gave him a two finger salute.

"Ay, how's it goin' my dude?" Gustavo announced like a trumpet from behind.

"Gustavo!" Gabriel exclaimed as he bro-hugged Gustavo.

"Good to see you my man."

"You too... man," Gabriel said, softly punching Gustavo's chest.

"Where have you been, bro?"

"Just—you know."

"Look, you don't even have to tell me. But tell me this—The next time you are going to be leaving for so long, please promise to tell me, okay?" Gustavo said, "I'm serious bro, I'm at the cafe every day just thinking like, 'when is Gabriel coming already?'"

"Aw, I appreciate that, and I'll be sure to tell you— Except that I probably won't be going anywhere again,"

Gabriel replied, "But man, the cafe—I miss that place. How's business been?"

"You know I'm just, everyday trying to make things better there and it's really becoming a good cafe, you know? Are you asking because you need some work?"

"Uh—Well actually that'd be nice. Would you really do that for me?"

"Bro, of course," Gustavo said enthusiastically, "Anything for you my friend."

"Well... sweet!" Gabriel exclaimed.

"Yeah man, just come by any day and we will figure something out for you."

"Dude—thank you Gustavo. Seriously."

"Ay, no problem, man," Gustavo said, placing his hand on Gabriel's shoulder.

"I'm gonna go say hi to my friend, but I'll for sure get back to you on this subject," Gabriel said.

"All right my dude," Gustavo said whimsically, pointing his fingers at Gabriel. "—You're the man."

Gabriel headed to Noah who was standing awkwardly in the hall.

"Hey bro, you'll never believe—I think I just got a job," Gabriel spoke up.

"That's sick dude," Noah responded, his gaze caught on something straight ahead, "—But have you ever seen such a pretty girl before?" He pointed down the hall. Gabriel realized Noah was pointing at Esther.

Esther was introducing herself to Leon and Mel just after she walked through the front door. Noah was saying things, but Gabriel couldn't have tuned him out more. This moment felt too surreal for Gabriel. After only seeing Lily in his dreams, he wasn't sure if he was ready to meet her again. His world froze as he felt his heart try to beat its way out of his chest. Gabriel glared at the door where Esther walked through, his focus undivided.

Then she walked in, Lily. She was carrying all of her elegance and peacefulness with her smile as she joined Esther in saying hi to Leon and Mel. Even the way she shook hands, made Gabriel melt. All the feelings from before came rushing in, and Gabriel became frail. He took a few steps towards her, and Lily noticed. He had no idea what Lily thought of him, or what she'd say, but he proceeded nonetheless. Esther lightly pushed Lily, encouraging her to come up to Gabriel, and Lily did. She walked slowly, and every daydream Gabriel ever had of Lily flashed before his eyes, but none of them compared to the real thing.

There were no words exchanged, but they both knew that they had moved on from what happened before. Gabriel moved his head to the side, indicating that he wanted Lily to follow him. She took his open hand and let him lead her outside. They walked through the hall, walking past his goldfish Atlas, and into the backyard where there was a trail. They calmly strode down the trail for a while. At the end of that trail was a tree with a bench under it, and it over-looked a pond that inhabited thousands of lily pads.

Gabriel and Lily both sat down on the bench made for two, him on the left and her on the right. They were completely alone. He handed her his journal, and opened the cover. Lily appeared exuberant as she beheld the works of art. She flipped through each page, taking just the right amount of time to appreciate each piece. When she turned the final page, revealing the tree that Gabriel had drawn, the one they were currently sitting under, she smiled contently. Gabriel thought to himself.

"I get it now; I know why Lily didn't fall for me like I did her. It was because she was too smart to give her love away to a heart as empty as mine. I guess one cannot love, if one does not first know love."

"Hey, listen," Lily spoke up. She closed the journal and handed it back to Gabriel. "Maybe we should get back to the house."

"Yeah… People actually came to see me—can you believe it?" Gabriel sighed. Lily smiled, but Gabriel could see that it was a half-hearted smile. He wanted to ask her what's wrong, but thought it best to not say anything at all. Right as Lily was about to get up to leave, Gabriel pulled out a paper from his pocket and placed it in her hand. Lily slowly unfolded the paper, revealing her phone number on it. It was the receipt that she handed him on the night they met.

"You see that number right there?" Gabriel asked. "It belongs to a girl that I respect very much, and that I'm intrigued by. Do you think… that… if I asked her—with the intention to get to know each other better—that she would maybe let me treat her to a cup of coffee sometime? I know a place."

"I think that, whoever this girl is, would rather not have you call her yet," Lily responded nervously, "—but, simply be a friend to her."

"How can I, when she is the only person in the world I want to be more than just friends with?"

"Well, to that I would suggest you show her you mean what you say. If you really care about her so much, then your feelings will withstand the test of time."

"What you're saying is, if I remain in this continuous state of infatuation, without knowing if she feels the same about me or not, that she will eventually give 'us' a chance?" Gabriel asked.

"I think she would definitely give you a chance," Lily admitted.

Gabriel leaned in and kissed Lily on her cheek. Lily's eye's bloomed as she turned away blushing. She brought the receipt up to her lips and softly kissed it, then folded it and put it in Gabriel's sweater pocket before walking away. Gabriel opened his journal and put the pencil to the center of a new page. He kept it there for a while as he looked out at the water. He decided that Lily was worth the wait, and so, Gabriel was ready to fall for Lily again. He knew that if they could somehow find love for each other, it would be much like the very rain that fell when they met, deluged.

<u>The End</u>

Excerpt from the Gospel of Luke, chapter fifteen, verses eleven through thirty-two (ESV):

[11] *And he said, "There was a man who had two sons.* [12] *And the younger of them said to his father, 'Father, give me the share of property that is coming to me.' And he divided his property between them.* [13] *Not many days later, the younger son gathered all he had and took a journey into a far country, and there he squandered his property in reckless living.* [14] *And when he had spent everything, a severe famine arose in that country, and he began to be in need.* [15] *So he went and hired himself out to one of the citizens of that country, who sent him into his fields to feed pigs.* [16] *And he was longing to be fed with the pods that the pigs ate, and no one gave him anything.*

[17] *"But when he came to himself, he said, 'How many of my father's hired servants have more than enough bread, but I perish here with hunger!* [18] *I will arise and go to my father, and I will say to him, "Father, I have sinned against heaven and before you.* [19] *I am no longer worthy to be called your son. Treat me as one of your hired servants."'* [20] *And he arose and came to his father. But while he was still a long way off, his father saw him and felt compassion, and ran and embraced him and kissed him.* [21] *And the son said to him, 'Father, I have sinned against heaven and before you. I am no longer worthy to be called your son.* [22] *But the father said to his servants, 'Bring quickly the best robe, and put it on him, and put a ring on his hand, and shoes on his feet.* [23] *And bring the fattened calf and kill it, and let us eat and celebrate.* [24] *For this my son was dead, and is alive again; he was lost, and is found.' And they began to celebrate.*

[25] *"Now his older son was in the field, and as he came and drew near to the house, he heard music and dancing.* [26] *And he called one of the servants and asked what these things meant.* [27] *And he said to him, 'Your brother has come, and your father has killed the fattened calf, because he has received him back safe and sound.'* [28] *But he was angry and refused to go in. His father came out and entreated him,* [29] *but he answered his father, 'Look, these many years I have served you, and I never disobeyed your command, yet you never gave me a young goat, that I might celebrate with my friends.* [30] *But when this son of yours came, who has devoured your property with prostitutes, you killed the fattened calf for him!'* [31] *And he said to him, 'Son, you are always with me, and all that is mine is yours.* [32] *It was fitting to celebrate and be glad, for this your brother was dead, and is alive; he was lost, and is found.'"*

Theparableofgabriel.com